Midnight in the Witch's Kitchen

edited by L. A. Story

Alban Lake Publishing

Midnight in the Witch's Kitchen

First Printing
January 2020

Alban Lake Publishing
P.O. Box 141
Colo, Iowa 50056-0141 USA
e-mail: albanlake@yahoo.com

Visit www.albanlakepublishing.com for online science fiction, fantasy, horror, scifaiku, and more. Stop by our online bookstore at www.irbstore.co for novels, magazines, anthologies, and collections. Support the small, independent press and your First Amendment rights.

Rise up, witches of the world and beyond! You have nothing to lose but your cauldrons!

Contents

Stories

Poetry

A note from the editor...

So... I pitched this crazy idea to Alban Lake's Tyree Campbell last year.

"Hey, I have this idea for a witch-themed anthology, but I want the short stories to have a certain feel to them. I can't explain it, I'll just know what I'm looking for when I see it. Also, it will have poetry—but not just any poetry—only poetry that rhymes because I'm looking for a spell-like quality. Oh, and did I mention I'm including a handful of recipes in the back from 'Granny's Kitchen'?"

I know he had to have thought I was completely off my rocker.

But, he and the wonderful folks at Alban Lake, Karen and Bill, gave me free rein to make it happen and I can't thank them enough.

They put their confidence in me. Well, then the talent search began. The call for submissions.

Oh, and so many answered the call for this quirky project. I read over a huge number of submissions over the course of several months. I didn't close the submissions until I had filled the slots I was allowed with the kind of stories I felt hit the mark of what I wanted.

These pages are filled with some very talented writers.

The idea for "Midnight in the Witch's Kitchen" was inspired by a character from my novel "The Witch of Hadler's Woods." In the book, I even have a chapter called Midnight in the Witch's Kitchen. My short story, The Whisperer, is a little story about the origins of Ruby Barnes (a.k.a. Granny Barnes in the novel) and a witch named Raven Miller. I was so enchanted by Granny Barnes—a matronly grandmother who feeds the masses in her kitchen by day, but at night, people come to her door for a wholly different reason. She does divinations, blessings, spells for prosperity, luck, love, or whatever thing of which someone might have need. She's a unique lady and if one wants those services, one can knock on her door only after the clock strikes midnight.

With that in mind, I wanted interesting tales that reminded me of the mystery surrounding witches.

I hope you enjoy the result of a crazy idea that just wouldn't go away.

Cheers,

LA

The Flying Spell
E. M. Eastick

I'd rather like to be a bird,
And so I wrote a spell,
That if you follow to the word,
Will have you flying well.

You'll need a pot of buckled tin,
A funnel long and hollow,
A golden spoon for stirring in,
Ingredients to follow:

A breath of wind from paradise,
A feather from a Roc,
A chili pepper for the spice,
The toe from Merlin's sock.

A ground-up periwinkle shell,
A splash of Captain's Rum,
A lock of hair from Tinkerbell,
A chewed-up piece of gum.

A clump of matted squirrel fur,
Three days beside the road,
Gold, frankincense, and myrrh,
A fat and warty toad.

A pinch of freshly fallen snow,
A leaf from autumn past,
Stir in southern salmon roe,
And stir it really fast.

Three scales from the mamba snake,
A baby dragon's wing,
A cup of water from the lake
That freezes in the spring.

The whiskers from a leopard seal,
Some plankton from the sea,
A freshly grated lemon peel,
A squished up bumble bee.

Boil the contents of the pot,
And whistle 'Help Me, Rhonda.'
If the mixture isn't hot,
Then boil a little longer.

Measure out a careful quart,
And gulp it down in one,
Dance a jig and think a thought,
And then the spell is done.

Jump off a roof and shout your name,
And let yourself be free.
Didn't work? Now that's a shame,
It worked okay for me.

Marigold at Midnight
Tyree Campbell

For Marigold Tallgrass there was something outré about having to descend three steps to enter the cottage after crossing the threshold. Above her the open rafters, ripe with webs and insect carcasses, only added to the otherness. The cottage could not have pleased her more.

She stood her carrybag on the dusty floor and took out five hurricane lanterns, chosen for their deep candlewells because the flames risked igniting the dust. These she placed strategically in the front room so that they formed the points of a pentagram. One by one she lit them with long matches. At first the flames flickered. Shadows appeared to move at the periphery of the room, and enhanced the ambience. Presently the flames steadied, and the shadows stilled once more. Standing in the center of the pentagram, Marigold clapped her hands three times. The sharp reports echoed throughout the empty house, and cautioned demons that their mistress was home from her long absence.

"Athwart," she called out.

There was no response, not even telepathic.

Well, she couldn't blame her familiar for being snooty. Not since birth had they been separated for so long. She pulled a soft leather pouch from her carrybag and loosened the drawstrings.

"I brought you some dried, honey-dipped locusts," she called out, a melodic, teasing summons.

Still not a sound came from within the cottage. The silence weighed on her heart.

"Maybe I should give them to Coralie," she muttered, tightening the strings. "Her raccoon will eat almost anything."

Wait.

A shadow edged low along the hallway wall and paused at the entrance to the front room as if in anticipation.

You could have left sooner.

The tone was heavy with accusation. "Yes," Marigold admitted. "I could have woven a spell and opened the cell door at any time. But I would have had to stay on the move, forever, as an escaped convict. This way, I served my sentence, and now I'm free." She sighed. "I missed you, Athwart."

The mottled brown coatimundi padded into the front room. *Let's see those locusts.*

She placed three on the antique coffee table, and Athwart leaped onto the sofa. After settling herself, she picked up one between her front paws, sniffed it, and purred with satisfaction.

"I thought you'd like those," said Marigold, as she took her carrybag to the bedroom and unloaded the clothing into the hamper. "They're almost as good as the food in jail."

Next time, don't interfere.

"I know, I know. But the poor man's coffee was cold." She returned to the front room. "I just used too strong a spell, and the cup fell onto his lap, and he testified that I deliberately spilled it on him."

Thirty days.

"I'm sorry. But it was only twenty. Good behavior, you see."

A second locust went down crunching. *It seemed like thirty.*

Marigold wanted to cry. "Oh, don't go on at me, Athwart. I said I was sorry." She forced herself to brighten as she sat down beside the coatimundi and stroked her back. "Did we have any visitors?"

Two seagulls. And Baywindow showed up.

Marigold laughed. "Belinda. What did she want?"

A miracle.

Marigold sat up straight. "Uh-oh. That sounds like trouble."

It is. Are there any more?

"Not until you tell me what she wanted."

There's a man she likes. She wants to be thinner.

"That sounds like a Stephen King story. Well, I can do it, but I don't know whether I should. Tonight's the night, you know."

I know.

"You sound dubious."

Do I? I'll wager that's because I'm dubious. Marigold, a massive adjustment such as the one you're planning is bound to have repercussions. To say nothing of con-cussions. Didn't that jail sentence teach you anything?

"This cannot possibly harm anyone, Athwart. Why are you always so negative?"

Thus my name.

"All I want to do is help people learn how to get along."

Do-gooder. I would like more of those locusts, if you think you can emerge long enough from your saccharine dreams to place some more on the table.

Smiling tolerantly, she complied. "And it has to be done at midnight."

Why this midnight?

She ruffled the fur at the top of Athwart's head. "Because it's the full moon, silly."

Marigold closed her eyes and sensed the time—Greenwich Mean, adjusted to local. Four hours and twenty-seven minutes to go. Plenty of time. After a nudge to Athwart to follow her, she went out the dinette door to the deck that gave onto the rugged Pacific coastline south of Carmel, forty yards away and ten yards below. She crossed her arms on the railing and leaned forward, relaxed. The sun was an hour from its nightly immersion. Sometimes she pretended she could hear it hiss as it touched the ocean at the horizon. Presently her chest rose and fell in a sad sigh. She wished there were someone to whom she might describe the sunset—or better yet, to share one with.

Marigold Tallgrass was hardly the sort of stereotype one might conjure upon hearing the word "witch." No hooked nose and chin, no cackle, not for her. To be sure, now and then she did use a broom for transportation—avoiding the TSA and the inevitable questions about the unusual objects in her carrybag; eyes of newt, for one—and she did employ a cauldron on occasion, albeit mostly for a homemade soup that both she and Athwart enjoyed. She was tall and slender—she liked to think of it as willowy—with hair now flaxen due to a spell—next week, umber! Her face, the fine pale white of *statuario* marble, took on a fresh glow after each shower, as if the loofa allowed her to polish her skin.

Her eyes, for the moment, were pearl-gray. A spell to change the color? She con-sidered: what accessorized with umber hair? Green, perhaps. She had not had green eyes for over a century. Yes... this time a jade green. Or maybe serpentine. So many colors, and so little time...

Athwart was staring up at her. She lifted the coatimundi up onto the railing. "Better?" she asked.

Her familiar tightly clutched the railing. *You can fly. I cannot.*

"Just look at the sunset."

I see black and white. Rods only. You promised me cones. You said you knew a spell.

"I do know a spell. And I did promise. Please wait a little longer, my friend."

I'll just be right here, grousing. Are you going to change clothes?

She was wearing black jeans and an aqua pullover, her gentle contours only vaguely evident under them, and black loafers. A long gauze skirt afterwards, she thought. Mauve, with a purple peasant blouse.

Peasants come in all colors.

Marigold chuckled. "Ah... the sky is turning."

It is all fifty shades of gray to me.

"Not for long."

She placed a sheet of yellowed parchment on the railing, and summoned an inked nib to her slender fingers. The numbers came to her, a string of binary code that she had conjured and memorized during her most recent incarceration. It related to technological deprivation, something others in the cells had experienced, though not herself. A word had also come to her, not out of nowhere, but from a cellmate: interconnectedness. At first the word meant nothing to Marigold. The more she thought about it—and in that cell she had ample time to think—the more she decided that it meant far more than the selective definition usually attributed to it. It was in the very nature of things—of existence itself—that everything is connected. It had very little to do with "six degrees of separation."

The oxygen that she exhaled fifteen times a minute traveled to some other entity, some other life form: her cellmate, a butterfly, the head of lettuce growing in the fields outside Salinas, the goose migrating to or from Manitoba, and so on. The herring that a man on a German boat caught in the Baltic Sea went to a woman in a cannery on shore who cleaned them and gave them to another man for smoking, from which point the smoked herring went to the canning process, involving a machine designed and manufactured by other men and women... somewhere—men and women who probably opened the tins and ate the smoked herring. That, was inter-connectedness. In one way or another, every thing on the planet—including the very planet itself—was involved with every other thing.

This, then, was the source of her powers. The source of her (she smiled at this) sorcery. She, and so very few others on the planet, recognized this. She, and she alone—or so she thought—knew what now had to be done. Because there was another kind of interconnectedness, a technological one, and it was destroying humanity.

The solution had come to Marigold in a flash—the way all good ideas come. The imposition of it would be hard on people at first, but people had endured and even thrived under such conditions. She considered relationships. Social media were no place to make friends. You needed to hear each other's words, not read them. Reading eliminated timbre and tone, accent and cadence. Eyes spoke volumes without so much as a consonant. And touch. My stars, touch! So she'd had her flash.

She tittered at the memory. "Eureka."

Athwart sneered. *You no smell-a so good yourself.*

The code was long, with many a winding turn that led to who knew where or when... but Marigold had engaged a memory spell that allowed her to recall it exactly, precisely, at any time. This was a Good Thing, as the trouble that a misplace 1 or 0 might cause... she shuddered to think. As in all spells, precision was required. The attraction spell she had cast on Gerrold Teasnake back in eighth grade even now, two centuries later, continued unabated, and his advances had been rejected by more than 32,500 girls and women. It was worse than being a small-press writer. And the spell had been intended to make *her* attractive to *him.* She sighed at the memory, and thought, *the best plans of mice and men to get laid...*

Athwart's tail rose. *That's not the right quote.*

"It is for me, my friend." She gazed out at the sunset. Red sky at night, sailor's delight. She'd known a few sailors, now and then. Even Captain James Cook, before he became the main course at the *Honolulu Snack & Hula.* The spell she'd cast on him served him right; dinner and a drink had been okay, but what he'd assumed would follow—not okay. And there was that problem with those growths on his toes...

Invited by nightfall, the stars came out, igniting in turns. Even this late in February, bits of the winter constellations took shape. A glimpse of Sirius, the Dog Star. Above her, dependable Arcturus. And Vega, poised to become the North Star in ten more millennia. She wondered whether she would be around to see that. There were longevity spells... but there was also a price.

Marigold snapped her fingers, and a spark formed that hovered just over her shoulder, allowing her to see the parchment and what she inscribed on it. Athwart blinked, and turned her face away.

Ones and zeroes she began to print, clearly and carefully, on the parchment. The ink did not run, but dried immediately. The code was much too long to fit across the parchment, or even across thirty of them, so she doubled it back in the ancient Linear B style, left to right for the odd-numbered lines, right to left for the evens, thus creating one continuous sequence. Small she printed, each numeral no larger than an eleven-point. Even with that size, she used up the entire sheet, leaving but a quarter-inch or so all around. At twenty minutes to midnight, she inscribed the last 1.

Light from the full moon overwhelmed that from the stars like cosmetic foundation over freckles: the stars were present, but no longer visible. The spark she had created still lurked over her shoulder, awaiting any further bidding she might have for it. Athwart, bored, had gone inside to watch a culinary show involving unusual foods. Marigold looked up. The Man in the Moon seemed to wink at her, knowing what she was about.

Eight minutes. Six. Three.

Marigold laid a Palmetto on the railing and enabled it.

The clock in the top right corner confirmed the accuracy of her own time forecast. Two minutes and twenty-seven seconds, and counting down. The monitor also showed the date, with the month and year. It also indicated that she had no messages pending.

So what else is new?

She draped the parchment over the railing. The spell required the light from the sun to ignite the parchment, even though the ignition had to be performed at midnight. The Moon reflected sunlight. From a pocket of her jeans she withdrew a magnifying glass. She turned the handle this way and that until the lens formed a tight spot of light. She waited.

Fifty-seven seconds.

She drew a full breath and held it for a couple beats before she expelled it. Thus relaxed, she steadied the glass in her hand. Time counted, unabated. The people of the world would wake up to better lives as they had to connect to one another in real time. Her gift to them. They would never know who had bestowed it on them, but that scarcely mattered to Marigold.

Thirty seconds. She aimed the dot of light at the parchment. Heat accumulated. Fifteen. A dark dot began to form on the parchment. Eight. The dot began to emit wisps of smoke. Four. One. The dot burst into flame.

The parchment burned. Marigold watch the Palmetto monitor. Nothing was happening there. Her heart lurched. Something was wrong. A zero? A one? Or did she have to wait until the entire parchment was ashes?

Ye goddesses...

C'mon, she urged the Palmetto and the flames. C'mon. I can save the world...

Plus thirty-two seconds. The parchment was ash. On the monitor, time kept on running without pause into the future. She stared at it in disbelief. Nothing had changed.

Nothing.

The stars held to their courses, the Moon man still watched her—perhaps with a sardonic smile now. A breeze blew. Waves frothed in the distant ocean. And all personal communication devices on the planet still operated. She had failed. She shed a tear, and another. Failure left her without even the strength to dry her cheeks. Blinking formed more tears.

I was so sure…

Loneliness set in, adding to her inability to change anything in the world. It would continue on, oblivious to her efforts, to her hopes. She had no friends to console her. Well, maybe one.

"Athwart," she called.

A man emerged onto the deck. Taller than Marigold, he had a shock of loose yellow hair and eyes like Venus in the morning. He was older, and he was naked. He was grizzled and gorgeous and had a sour expression on his face. "I can't believe you fed me locusts," he said. "Don't you have anything better to give me?"

She did.

Gator Girl

Sarah Cannavo

Most of the gator was still submerged under the murky, moss-frothed swamp water, but its nostrils and hooded yellow-green eyes had broken the surface and it stared up at Caleb. He held his gun at the ready but otherwise stood as still as the cypress trees around him. Sweat cut through the dirt on the back of his neck. His catch that day, a fat possum, lay against his left boot. He'd spent the day tracking, hunting, and had been heading home through the humid early evening when the water had shifted with a hiss he'd recognized at once and drawn his gun against.

He didn't want to kill the gator, but if the bastard made a move he wouldn't let himself get dragged under easy. He waited, finger near the trigger, while carnival shades of pink and orange streaked the August sky as the sun settled lower and made the shadows of tree roots writhe like rattler nests kicked into a frenzy. The gator hissed again, long slender snout opening on craggy prehistoric teeth. Caleb's finger caressed the trigger.

Easy. Easy...

"Hey now. We don't need any of that."

His concentration broke from the alligator as a woman's voice rang through the swamp, firm but not unkind, like a mama breaking up squabbling brothers in the yard. About ten yards away she stood, tall and pale in a short white dress, with a nest of long blonde curls and bare feet caked in mud, hands on her shapely hips.

And if that wasn't odd enough, Caleb watched as she started walking across the water towards him and the alligator. No, not across the water, Caleb realized, but across the backs of other gators lining up for her like it was the most natural thing in the world, each one swimming away again once she'd stepped to the next. Caleb blinked, but the sight didn't change, and when the woman finally stepped onto the sandy soil beside him she placed a slender hand on his rifle barrel and pushed it gently down. He was so stunned he let her, watching mutely as she said in a voice like a clear flowing stream, "It's all right, hon. You won't need that."

She looked down at the gator Caleb's gaze had been locked with, voice sterner now. "Haven't I told you to leave people alone? Go on now, git."

And to cap the moment, the alligator slunk away with what, if Caleb didn't know better, he'd have called a defeated expression, scaled body submerging and towing white ripples in its wake. "There," the woman said, smiling, turning back to Caleb. "Sorry 'bout that. I try to keep 'em in check, but they do get outta line sometimes."

"Uh-huh," Caleb grunted, staring.

The simplest explanation was that he was hallucinating, that while he was retrieving the possum some overlooked root had snagged his boot and he'd tumbled, struck his head on a stone and started dreaming as he bled out. Or maybe he *had* made it home and drank some of that rank-ass shit his useless brothers were always brewing, and this was all some cheap 'shine dream. Swamps were strange ground, sure, and every member of his family and everyone he met who ventured in regularly had at least one tale to tell of things they'd seen, heard, or experienced but couldn't explain. Caleb had a few of his own. But, beautiful blonde women didn't walk across gators and talk to others. Surreptitiously Caleb's fingers probed under his shaggy brown hair, feeling for a wound, finding none.

"You live around here?" the woman asked. Up close Caleb judged her somewhat younger than him—early or mid-thirties, maybe, long-legged and fine-featured, with an earthy scent to her skin and an openness in her eyes and expression no one back home had, even the kids.

Caleb considered her a moment, then grunted again and shrugged one muscled shoulder. "Close enough. Prob'ly won't make it home by dark, but I can find somewhere to hole up."

Panic flooded those guileless eyes. "Dark?" The woman flung her gaze around, took in the lengthening shadows dripping down to the dark water, the growing shades of violet and blue blooming on the horizon. "Oh, Jesus, I lost track of time." She grabbed Caleb's hand and tugged.

"C'mon, we gotta go."

Caleb tore his hand away. "What? I ain't going anywhere with you, ma'am."

"Please." Everything about her begged him, eyes and voice and body. She held out her hand again; around her wrist brown leather bracelets strung with beads and bone were knotted, and between them Caleb glimpsed the ink of a tattoo on her skin. "I know you don't know me, but it's not safe to be out here after dark. There's much weirder shit than me out here—weirder and worse. I don't care how well you know the swamp; if you stay out here you won't make it home. You need to come with me. *Please.*"

Caleb studied her a minute more, read the genuineness of her fear. Something had spooked a girl who walked on gators' backs, and Caleb felt some twitch of instinct scurry through his gut like a spider. "All right," he said eventually, slinging his gun over his shoulder and letting her take his hand again. "I'll go with you."

Relief washed over her face. "C'mon." Caleb barely had time to snag his possum before the woman was off and moving like hounds were snapping hungry at their heels.

Caleb had grown up in this chunk of Louisiana, had been tracking, trapping, and hunting in it since he could walk. He knew its ways well, and the one thing his pa'd ever been proud of him for was his wilderness skills. But this weird woman made her way through the darkening swamp like no one he'd ever seen, never a wrong footfall, never snagged by a creeper or tripped up by the deceptive landscape, with no more light than what filtered from the honey-gold crescent moon down through the cypress and wax myrtle leaves. She seemed half a ghost, wild and luminous, as she led him on, and only the inarguably solid feel of her warm white hand in his proved he wasn't being drawn by a haint.

She didn't speak except to urge him to hurry or watch his step; strain rode her expression the whole way, and she seemed alert for something beyond the chorus of croaking frogs and calling night-birds starting their performance on schedule. Maybe it was just runoff from her, but Caleb sensed something as well, in the hollows of his shoulder blades, the hair on his arms, the pit of his stomach. It was as if the swamp itself was holding its breath, waiting for something to happen.

Shit, don't let her spook ya, Caleb told himself.

"There." She smiled finally. "We're home."

Up ahead rose a small cabin—a shack, really, but well-built from logs and thatched with a palm-frond roof, girdled with trumpet vine and spider lily. Rusty Louisiana iris and cardinal flower plants grew around it and a wooden canoe lay overturned at the foot of a water oak tree whose branches bore chimes of colored glass shards. As the pair approached, warm amber light flared behind the curtained windows, flickering—candle- or lantern-light, Caleb figured.

"It ain't much, but it's nice here." She wiped her bare feet on a woven mat outside the door. "Try not to track too much—" She glanced back, taking in the grime caked on Caleb's clothes and skin. "Well, wipe your feet, at least."

Inside, the cabin was snug and smelled of candle wax and flowers—not surprisingly, as bunches of dried herbs and flowers hung on the walls and sat on shelves amid cans and jars of food, and bouquets of wildflowers sat in other ribbon-wrapped jars around the place, and candles burned in cracked china saucers to greet them. How they'd been lit, Caleb couldn't and wouldn't think.

A rabbit-pelt rug warmed the floor by the rumpled bed; small, rough crystals of various colors rested amid bits of animal bones and wood chunks carved with strange symbols on windowsills and the small table against the wall. "Make yourself at home," the woman said, cleaning away a heap of crumpled clothes. "Sorry 'bout the mess; I would've cleaned if I knew I was gonna have a guest, but Momma had the visions. I'm just a regular conjure-woman."

"So you're a swamp witch," Caleb said, standing on the room's edge, looking around. "Like that Misty Day chick?"

The woman looked up. "Who?"

"TV character." He peered at a fox skull on a shelf, its dark hollow sockets staring back.

"I wouldn't know." She continued neatening as she spoke, smiling. "Momma raised me out here, and there aren't too many cable guys willin' to make the trip."

Caleb snorted. She looked at him, white smile growing. "You don't believe I'm a witch, do you? Even after what you've seen?"

Caleb shrugged, turning away to study a feather-edged dream-catcher dangling on the wall. "People believe in hoodoo. That don't make it real, though. I once saw a guy charm a snake at a county fair. That magic, too?" He picked up a pale purple crystal, feeling its weight in his palm. "This your banishing crystal?"

She looked at him like the dumbest creature on God's green earth. "Any crystal's a banishing crystal if you hurl it hard enough."

He set it down. "True."

He heard her move behind him. "I'll prove myself," she said, and the feel in the cabin changed. It was like the air before a bolt of lightning broke it, thick and tense with sparks. After a moment she spoke, voice lower, more subdued. "The gators didn't get your uncle TJ."

Caleb stiffened, hot wires running through his skin. "What?"

"Well, they did, but only after you did. He'd lost his job and your dad let him stay in your trailer, didn't he? He'd been there a few weeks before he started coming to where you slept."

Caleb whirled on her. "Shut up."

Her eyes were shocked, sorrowful. "You wanted him to stop. He took you fishing, and you made him stop."

Ten years old, coming up behind his uncle, pressing the black gun barrel to the back of his head and squeezing the trigger. The boom had echoed through the trees, scaring a heron into flight; blood and brains had painted Caleb's face. He'd cut the body into messy chunks and thrown them into the water, then run home screaming about an overturned boat, a hungry gator. His miraculous escape was recounted in family lore to this day.

He grabbed the witch, shook her hard, stomach roiling and blood boiling. "I said shut up!"

"I'm sorry," she said. "I didn't go looking for—I can't control what comes to me."

He broke away, breathing heavy, grunting as he rubbed his mouth with the back of his hand. "I'm sorry," she said again, seeming to mean it, for all the good it did.

He pointed at her. "You pull that shit again I'll kill you,

get it? Stay outta my goddamn head."

She held her hands up. "I promise."

Slowly Caleb calmed, breathing ragged but evening. Watching him carefully, the witch said, "I'd like to feed you, but I didn't get a chance to check my traps today."

Caleb held up the possum by the tail. "This do?"

She smiled.

"What's your name, anyway?" Caleb asked, licking grease from his fingers and tossing away the gnawed bone he held.

"Allie," she said.

He stared at her. "No it ain't."

She grinned. "Portia. My name's Portia."

Caleb's brow furrowed. "Like the car?"

She laughed. "Like the Shakespeare character. 'My little body is aweary of this great world' and all that."

"Never read him."

"Momma loved him. She was a very well-read witch." Portia gestured to a few crooked book stacks where tattered volumes of Shakespeare and Jane Austen were jumbled among titles Caleb couldn't decipher. "She moved out here before I was born, raised me up, taught me about my powers. I can cast spells, read people and animals, talk to 'em, like you saw—though I don't know if it's the words they respond to so much as the power behind 'em. I had a snake once, sweetest little thing in the world. Used to sleep curled up right at the foot of my bed. I called her Kitten."

"And your dad?" Caleb asked. "What was he?"

Portia smiled. "Momma always said he was an asshole."

"I think our dads might've worked together, then." Caleb sat straighter, wiping his hands on his jeans. "All right, Portia, time to stop pussyfooting around. What the hell's out there that even a witch like you's afraid of? What'd you drag me back here for?"

Portia set down the jar of dark muscadine wine they'd been sipping from and drew her knees up to her chest. "You hear about them people goin' missing or dyin' in the swamp, Caleb? Over the last month or so?"

Caleb nodded. Hunters, tourists, people who lived in the area, all had been disappearing; if they were found it was as bloody bones and scraps of flesh. "They're blaming cougars, gators, the usual suspects."

"It's not." Portia hugged herself tighter. "It's a rougarou. You know what that is?"

"Cajun wolfman," Caleb said. "When I was a kid my brothers'd take turns putting on this cheap-ass wolf mask and scratching at my window screen, whisperin' the rougarou would get me when I fell asleep. Scared the shit outta me when I was five." He scratched his chin. "You want me to believe there's one stalking the swamp now?"

"I don't care if you believe me or not; I saw it." All levity—and color—had fled Portia's face, bleaching her white as the bones on her shelves; tall as she was, the way she curled in on herself, the naked fear in her eyes, made her seem small, vulnerable, and an uncomfortable familiarity rippled in Caleb's gut—back in that goddamn trailer, begging his pa for the first and last time not to go out hunting, not to leave him alone, Pa shoving him away and rasping in his guttural, Marlboro-accented bark, *Quit yer bitchin', you little pussy. You want me to stay here or you wanna eat? Besides, you ain't alone. Uncle TJ'll look after ya til your brothers 'n I get back.* The look Portia wore now was the same Caleb'd seen in the trailer's cracked mirror as the screen door slammed behind his father and brothers, the same look he'd worn until he'd slid the gun out from under his pa's pillow, felt its weight, tucked it into his waistband and gone fishing with Uncle TJ. It was raw, deep, gutting fear. Caleb's skin crawled.

"When?" he asked, muscadine wine lying heavy on his tongue.

Portia's voice shook. "Two weeks ago. I was out at night gathering some moss and mushrooms when the wind changed and I smelled blood, fresh blood, a lot of it. Thick enough to choke you." Her eyes met Caleb's, said silently they both knew what that was like. "I was worried, I thought maybe someone was hurt, or an animal was, so I tracked the scent. I came out of the brush down the river, and there it was, across the water—there *he* was.

"I got lucky; his back was to me, and he didn't notice

me. Too busy, I guess." She wound a curl around her finger, tugged; as she spoke sensations passed through Caleb, as though he'd been there as well or she was taking him there: the steaming air, the croak of frogs and the splash of black water, the hot copper tang of blood in his nose and throat. "He was eating—devouring, more like; there was a man's corpse on the ground in front of him, and the way he was tearing into it made how we dug into that possum look like royal manners. And he—Jesus, he was a beast, pure 'n simple. Not human, not animal, but the worst of both. He was hunched on two legs, covered in this brown fur matted with mud and blood, and he had this long, thick tail swinging behind him, these godawful paws... . And when I saw him, saw what he'd done to that man, I knew. I knew he was the one that was takin' and killin' those people. I could sense it, you know? I don't know if it was magic or what, but I could.

"I was terrified. I was so fuckin' scared I forgot I was a witch." Portia gave a chuckle shaky as a candle flame in the wind. "I can only imagine Momma's face if she ever heard that. She wasn't scared of anythin'. Not that I ever saw, anyway. But I turned tail and ran all the way home. At one point I heard him howlin' clear across the swamp, and it was the worst thing I'd ever heard in my life. I heard it some nights since then, and I'm not ashamed to tell you it's come up in my nightmares, too. I made this place safe, but that don't mean much when the monster's already inside your head."

Her lips curled in a small, self-deprecating smile as she sniffled and wiped away the tears she'd only just seemed to notice glistening on her cheeks. Caleb realized sweat had broken out on his skin; he had the notion he should try to comfort Portia somehow, say something, go sit with her, put an arm around her, something. But he'd never been good at shit like that, and, feeling awkward, he did the only thing he could think to do, passing the wine jar back to her; she sniffled and smiled again. "Thanks," she said, sipping. Afterwards, voice stronger, she said, "A witch's curse can make a man a rougarou, and his bite can make others like him. That's why I didn't want you out there, gettin' killed or bitten."

"Appreciate it." Caleb flicked his hair out of his eyes. "But you said you saw this thing two weeks ago? What've you been doin' since then? I mean, you got some kinda plan, or are you just gonna cower in here every night hopin' the big bad wolf don't getcha?"

Portia glared, candle flames flaring higher. "Course not, dumbfuck. First thing I did when I got home that night was ward this place against it. Then I gathered the ingredients I needed for the spell I found; that took some time. And the animals have standing orders to look out for this thing, but he don't show himself every night—least, not around here."

"Spell? To do what?"

"Hopefully, I can save him. I'm scared, not heartless."

"*Save* him?"

Portia got up, lifted a small wooden box and showed Caleb the contents: a pouch of earth, candles carved with symbols, bits of bones and chalk, all incomprehensible to him. "Cursed or bitten, a rougarou changes every night, and a lot of them don't remember what they become once they turn human again in the morning. It might not be this guy's fault, what he's done. I don't know what spell was put on him, or if he was bit, so I can't reverse it. But I found a spell that reveals a person's true nature, and if I can catch him and cast it, I think it should turn the rougarou human again."

"Yeah?" Caleb stood, shutting the box. "And what if that don't work, Sabrina?"

"Then I'll have to kill him." Portia set her jaw.

Caleb shook his head. "Not without me, you ain't."

Portia glowered. "You don't think I can handle it."

"Honestly, I don't know if you can or can't. Tonight's been too damn strange for me to even start making sense of right now. But if there's a monster out in the swamp I'm not gonna just sit back here scratchin' my balls. I'm gonna do something about it."

After a moment Portia smiled. "All right. Thank you, Caleb."

He nodded and started, "So how do we find this th—"

A howl cut through the darkness, sudden and swift as a bullet to the back. There was something of the wolf to it, and something of a man, but the combined effect was of something entirely other, alien, *wrong,* a violation of some kind, forcing itself on the normal pattern of the night. Caleb's balls tried to retreat into him; he looked at Portia, demanded "That it?" though he knew it was. There was nothing else it could be.

The witch'd lost what color she'd regained; her "Uh-huh" was a wisp insubstantial as foxfire.

The echoes rang in Caleb's ears. "That was close. It's out there now."

"Can you tell how close? Do you see anything?"

Caleb crossed to the window, peered through the glass as his skin prickled and the hair on his arms, the back of his neck, stiffened. His gaze swept the dark, adjusting to it, discerning the water oak, the canoe, shadows among shadows. "Nah, there's noth—"

The face surfaced out of the blackness, pressing itself to the glass opposite Caleb. He stumbled back, blood freezing and eyes locked to it, as behind him Portia cried out in shock. It was no cheap rubber mask; it was a living, breathing beast, brown-furred and yellow-eyed, leering at the pair with its tongue protruding from a leathery snout full of jagged fangs. The rougarou stood on two legs, over six feet tall, and as its gaze devoured the humans it let out a slavering half-laugh, half-snarl that cut through Caleb's spine, brutal, guttural, hungry.

Caleb dove for his gun, cursing—how'd he not heard it approach? "It can't get in, Caleb," Portia said, and just as the creature's claws scrabbled against the window symbols etched in fire flared on the glass, driving it back with yelp.

"Bastard must've tracked our scents." Caleb jacked a round into the chamber as the rougarou renewed its assault, battering walls, the front door, hard enough to shake books and skulls from the shelves even as it howled in pain, protection spells searing its skin. "What now, Portia?"

"This," she said, and the air changed again, Caleb's skin prickling in recognition. As he watched, Portia's eyes glowed with rings of white light, arms raising like slow-spreading wings, and she began chanting, voice rising like a tide, swelling with every syllable. She shouted the last word and symbols glowed on walls and windows, some unseen force hurling the rougarou against the water oak to crumple among its roots.

"He won't stay down for long. Give me your gun."

Caleb did, one eye on the unmoving rougarou. Portia gripped the rifle, eyes closed, and murmured more liquid syllables; the gun shimmered around the edges, the same white like what'd gleamed in her eyes, and when it died she passed it back. "Those bullets should stop him, if it comes to that."

Caleb felt the gun cautiously, expecting to feel heat or some sort of sensation, but there was only the warmth Portia's hands had left. "All right, witchy-poo. Grab your shit and let's do this."

Portia snagged her spellbox and they stepped into the night. The steamy air carried the scent of her flowers, the rot of standing water, the somehow green scent of swamp mud—and overlaying it all an animal musk so strong Caleb's nose stung and his skin crawled. He kept his gun ready as they approached, in case the rougarou was playing possum, but he didn't move even when Caleb nudged his flank with his boot. "All right," Caleb said lowly, and Portia flew into action, hogtying the rougarou with surprising skill and speed.

Caleb stood guard as Portia drew a circle in the earth, surrounded by the carved candles and filled with similar symbols; long curls stirring in a breeze Caleb couldn't feel, she arranged bones, crystals, and a clump of matted fur she cut from the rougarou's tail within the circle. "It might work better if I had some of his clothes, too," Portia said, rubbing her hands together as she stood and the candles flared to life, brow creasing in worry.

"You make do with what you got," Caleb said, and she gave a small smile.

The wolfman stirred as Portia began chanting, chafing against his bonds, snarling and twisting on the ground. Caleb watched in horrified fascination, taking in the furred, muscled limbs, the wicked claws, the hot yellow eyes that roved like fire over the creature's captors. He thought of the missing and dead and prayed like hell Portia finished before the thing got loose.

Portia's voice rose over the rougarou's grunted, wordless

protests; as it crested light glowed around him, suffusing his fur, drowning out the amber drip of moonlight from above, and when it broke the rougarou's howl split the night and Caleb turned his head against the tidal wave of light.

The glow and Portia's triumphant look dimmed in the same moment. The rougarou still lay there, snapping and twisting in more of a frenzy than ever, baying madly at the hot black sky.

"I... I don't understand." Dropping to her knees she sifted, shaking, through the bric-a-brac she'd scattered in the circle, candle flames bowing as she moved. "I've never done this before, but I thought... Maybe I did something wrong."

A notion, heavy as lead, settled in Caleb's skull, sank to his stomach. "I don't think so," he said, hefting his gun again, looking down at the rougarou.

Portia looked up "What do you m—"

The rougarou burst up, bonds broken, and barreled into Portia, slavering and snapping for her throat. They tumbled tangled to the ground; before Caleb could fire Portia brought up a fist still clamped around a crystal and bashed it against the rougarou's skull. He reeled back with a wounded, hateful howl and bounded toward the brush on four long legs, thick tail flicking behind him; Caleb aimed and fired, heard a yelp before the wolfman disappeared into the trees.

Shit, winged him. Caleb rushed to Portia as she pushed herself up. "You all right?"

She stared at him, eyes hollow, haunted. He shook her, looking her over, searching for blood, broken skin. "Portia! C'mon. You all right? He bite you?"

She shook her head. "N... No, I'm all right." She gripped his arm, gaze snapping up to his. "When he hit me, I saw... I couldn't stop it... I saw what he's done, it all just came to me..." Portia looked sick; her nails dug into his skin. "Caleb, Christ, there's so much..."

He shook her again, more gently this time, his suspicion solidifying. "Hey, Portia. Snap outta it. You with me?"

Another moment and she returned to herself, nodding more solidly, bracelets clattering as she brushed dirt off her stained dress. "Yeah, I'm here. I just—I don't understand why that didn't work; he should be human now."

"Well, he ain't. But he's hurt." Caleb walked to the brush and found broken branches, droplets of blood splashed in an irregular rain on the dark ground. He grinned grimly. "I can track him, and we can end this shit."

No reply. Looking back, he saw Portia staring, pale and downcast, at the remnants of her circle. "I thought I could save him." She nudged a candle stub with her toe.

"Hey." Caleb walked back, tilted her chin up. "This ain't your fault, and it ain't the spell's, either. Before tonight I woulda said all this hoodoo was bullshit. Not now. You're a goddamn swamp witch, and you're a badass with that banishing crystal, too." She cracked a smile. "So we can't save him. You told me what that means."

"We gotta stop him." Portia nodded, sparks of light dancing in her irises. "All right, let's go."

A small ball of electric-green light illuminated their surroundings as they tracked the beast, Caleb's gun ready, the air around Portia crackling with energy. The swamp was unusually, unsettlingly still, that held-breath feeling again; the frogs had fallen silent, the owls and insects, and if it weren't for the paw prints in the mud and streaks of blood glistening here and there it might've seemed the hunter and witch were the only living things left in the world.

Branches snapped nearby. Portia started to whisper; Caleb held up a hand, cutting her off, looking around. Unseen, something splashed in the distance, a different direction than the soft footfalls behind them. The pair whirled, green light glowing brighter, throwing eerie shadows on the black landscape; nothing burst out at them, though, and the growls that slithered through the cypress came from ahead of them. Caleb's heart pounded; he and Portia shared a look, her pale face dotted with droplets of sweat. The rougarou was toying with them.

Blood glistened on a wax myrtle, wet against Caleb's fingertips. He grunted and waved Portia on, watching for yellow eyes in the dark, hearing once a long, throaty howl that curved to the moon and cut like a blade. As its echoes died away Caleb saw claw marks on a tree, fresh wounds, but his damp forehead creased as he touched them. They were high, even given the size of the creature.

What the hell—

It was as if—

"Portia, get back!" Caleb pushed her out of the way as the rougarou leapt snarling down from the tree, crashing onto Caleb. His muscles strained, hands buried in rank matted fur as he struggled to keep those dripping fangs from his flesh; in the depths of the eyes above him he saw no recognition that, during the day, they both wore human forms, just anger, madness, hate. The gun had been knocked away on impact; Caleb couldn't risk freeing a hand long enough to scrabble for it.

"Get the hell off him!"

Portia's shout rang like a rifle shot. The rougarou growled at her, Caleb crying out as claws sank into the meat of his left shoulder; his blood's copper tang mingled with the rancid steam of the rougarou's breath, and then the furred body atop his was ripped away by a wind scented with hyacinth and honeysuckle, moss and muscadine berries. Caleb's gaze whipped and found Portia with hands outflung, fingertips glowing, glaring at the rougarou as it rolled in the dirt. Her power was palpable; all fear had fled her expression. As the rougarou rose into the air, twitching and whimpering, the swamp witch was radiant, terrifying, utterly and unmistakably nobody to be messed with.

"Here's your shot, Caleb," she called, keeping the thrashing beast suspended.

Caleb moved, clutching his wounded shoulder; blood pumped and his muscles screamed in protest, but he picked up the fallen gun and forced his scarlet-stained hands to steady. He shot and didn't wing the creature this time; his skull exploded in a mass of ruined meat, last howl cut abruptly off.

Portia let the body drop; in the dirt it took a human form, face obliterated by the killing shot, a male with an anchor tattooed on one arm, body corded with muscle. Portia's attention diverted to Caleb, though. "Your arm—did he bite you?"

"Nah, just clawed me some." Caleb's breath caught as Portia's fingers probed the fiery cuts, a hiss trapped behind his teeth.

She looked up at him. "Sorry."

"Ain't your fault. You did your job."

"I'm wonderin' something," Portia said as she bandaged the cuts with a strip of fabric from the hem of her dress. "What did you mean earlier, when you said I hadn't done the spell wrong? He didn't change back."

"That spell reveals a person's true nature, right?" Portia nodded, finishing her rough patch job. "It did. Whoever that sonuvabitch was, he was a monster before that curse was laid on him. Only thing that changed was his shape. And you can't save a monster. Only thing you can do is stop 'em, and hopefully that'll save somebody else."

Portia was silent, absorbing this. Caleb, arm throbbing, walked to the corpse and grabbed a leg, and after a moment she came and hefted the other, and they started dragging.

When the pair reached the water's edge, the gators were already waiting. Caleb counted six in the green light, jaws parted, scaled bodies breaking the surface; he wondered if any of them was the one who'd stared him down what seemed an eon ago. Their grim work done, Caleb and Portia tossed the corpse into the water and left the gators to theirs.

Dawn was breaking when they reached the spot where they'd met yesterday, light bleeding back into the sky. They'd stopped back at Portia's cabin, where she'd applied a poultice to his cuts and laughed at the expression its smell caused, promising he'd heal in a few days.

"What are you gonna tell your brothers?" she asked now as they stopped.

Caleb shrugged, instantly regretted it. "Don't know. I'll think of somethin' on the way." He kicked at a clump of mud. "So will I, uh, see you around or anythin'?"

Portia smiled, brighter than the newborn sun. "You know where I live, Caleb." She pulled off one of her bracelets, slipped it around his wrist; a tingle travelled up his arm, and a familiar glow shivered faintly around it for a moment. "This'll help you find it again, if you ever want to." She leaned in and kissed his cheek, her lips soft and warm; when she pulled back she laughed again at the look on his face. "Come by if you're ever in the area."

"I will," he said, and he did.

Singular
Anatoly Belilovsky

I was a shadow of a waxwing slain
Whom witchcraft brought to life again,
I was a wing of the butterfly
For whom to live, a worm must die,
I was a furnace in whose soul
A flame is born of lumps of coal,
I was—I had—a present tense,
My futures in a fractured lens.
I know the genesis of my pain:
I love the drop but not the rain,
I love the bee but not the swarm,
I love the wave but not the storm,
I love the flower, not the lawn,
To *thou*, not to *you*, I'm drawn,
I love the fissure, not the wall,
I love the one.
I don't love all.

Aunt Helena

James Pate

The first time Roland noticed the difference in his house, he was coming in from moving a row of ferns to the back of his garden. As he stepped into the kitchen and walked toward the sink to wash his hands, he stopped and stared at the room around him: the counters, the oven, the lime-green walls. Usually when entering a house from the outside the air felt different. More enclosed, more compact. But here he sensed he was still outside, the walls and ceiling being nothing more than an illusion, an elaborate trick of light. The difference was subtle, but it was there, and it was persistent.

It did not go away as dusk fell. And it remained there the next morning.

A house that was no longer a house.

The first few days, he thought little of it. He chalked it up to tiredness, to bad nerves. (He had always had bad nerves. Even as a child, he'd had insomnia, staring at the night-black window near his bed for hours.) But the sense of living in a house he could see and touch but that was not actually there remained. He felt exposed. Unsheltered. Unmoored.

At night, in the dark, the sense of spaciousness was especially keen. Moving through the blackness of his bedroom and hallway toward the bathroom at the end of the landing, Roland felt as if he were moving through a wide meadow. Some nights he clicked his tongue, or called out a weak, "Hello." The sound would never strike right: it had a reverb suggesting much wider spaces. He'd put his hand out and touch the wall, the banister. Still there, he'd think. Still where he knew it should be, even if he felt he was outside, in the middle of the yard, with nothing but shifting, moon-etched clouds overhead.

In the bathroom, he would click on the light over the medicine cabinet. The sight of the massive tub and black tiled floor would reassure him.

Yet even here he sensed no enclosure. His eyes told him he was inside. His body and the inner workings of his brain whispered he was not.

After a week of this, he made up his mind to go into town and see if other buildings harbored a similar effect. Caleb, Louisiana was a twenty-minute drive away from his brick house in the woods. On the first of September, he dressed in clean un-muddied clothes, and drove his Ford truck to the Caleb Library, which set between a bakery and a tiny funeral home.

The moment he entered the building, with its stiff-faced portraits of town founders and towering book-shelves, he wanted to weep with relief. For the first time in days he was truly in a room again. He gripped the back of a chair at one of the reading tables and closed his eyes tight. He only opened them again when he heard a group of kids at a nearby table muttering about him. "Is he going to die?" asked a boy.

"Let's watch and find out," said a girl.

He met Elizabeth at Tommy's Diner, which stood across the street from the library. She was his one friend in the area. Like him, she was originally from New Orleans. Also like him, she was into the Tarot and magic and witchcraft, and they frequently traded the old crumbl-ing paperbacks about alchemy and Aleister Crowley.

"Something's wrong with my house, but if I tell you what it is, you're going to think I'm really losing it," he said.

"I thought you lost it long ago," Elizabeth said. "Don't you worry about that." She lifted her coffee mug, took a sip. She wore a short-sleeved black turtleneck and a chain with a silver cross and her long nails were painted green.

"When I'm inside my house, it's like it's not there," Roland admitted.

"Where does it go?"

"It doesn't go anywhere. I can still see it fine." He laughed uneasily. He went into detail about his recent experiences, starting with the morning he had moved the ferns and ending with his visit to the library. He added, "Peculiar thing is that I don't have that sense when I go anywhere else. So it can't be in my head. It's just my house. I go inside, and it seems like I'm still outdoors, in the middle of the yard."

Elizabeth placed her mug on the table. "Does the wind blow through the walls?"

He shook his head. "No. I know the walls are actually there. I'm not crazy. I just don't feel them anymore."

She tapped her fingernail on the lip of her mug. "Was it gradual or sudden?"

"Sudden. At least I think so. I woke up that morning, drank some coffee, read part of that book you lent me, and went outside to work on the garden. That morning, everything felt normal. It was only when I came back in at lunchtime that I noticed the difference."

"The book I lent you... you mean *Regina Ignis*?"

"That one, yeah."

She looked at him as if she expected him to say something more. When he didn't, she leaned forward, her arms crossed on the tabletop, and said, "I'll come over tomorrow afternoon, once I get off work. I'll check it out, see if I feel the same way when I go inside."

He nodded. "Thank you. Yes. That would be great."

"What did you think of the book? It took me a long time to track that one down."

Roland said, "I only got a few pages in. I think a lot of it is over my head. All those incantations about being the keeper of the flame—I had the sense there was some history to it I wasn't picking up on."

"Maybe there is. When I come by, I'll tell you what I know about it."

"Please do."

"And I'll check up on your house. See if it's trying to tell you something."

"It doesn't want me inside anymore. That's what I think it's trying to say."

They laughed, and drank from their mugs. A few sprinkles of late summer rain striking the window beside them.

The house and its seven acres of land had belonged to his aunt, who had been a writer of Gothic teen novels in the 1980s. Aunt Helena was no Judy Blume in terms of fame, but she was reasonably successful in those years. And she earned remarkably more than his father did as a butcher at Kroger's, and his mother, who owned a hair salon on Magazine Street.

Growing up, Roland liked his aunt even if he rarely saw her. At Christmas and Easter, she would show up in one of her flowing, floral-patterned dresses, her hair a wild mane of silver and orange, and smoke black cigarettes that smelled of hot asphalt at the family dining room table. But during the rest of the year it was as if she did not exist.

She did not get on with her sister. His mother. And she didn't get along well with his father, either. Roland was one note of discord between his aunt and parents.

"If he doesn't want to play with the other kids, don't force him," his aunt said after the Christmas meal one year. Up in his room playing with a train set, he could hear them downstairs, around the oak table.

His father's thick voice rose up through the house. "It's not healthy, him spending his days in his room, reading all the time. And those books he checks out from the library, all that shit about witches and Jack the Ripper... It's morbid. It can't be healthy."

"He takes after me. He has an imagination."

"Yeah, and all he does is live in it." His mother was speaking now. "A boy from school lives down the street, and every time he comes here, asking if Roland wants to play, Roland always makes up some excuse to stay inside, holed up with a book."

"Maybe the boy isn't worth playing with," his aunt answered. "Have the two of you ever considered that?"

On those holidays when his aunt came to the house, she would sometimes enter his room, sit on the edge of his bed, and give him a present wrapped in shiny paper. They were always books. Volumes by Poe, or Hoffman, or Jean Ray. One Easter morning she gave him Mary Shelley's *Frankenstein,* its illustration of the creature on the cover making him look less like Karloff and more like a Romantic poet. Curly locks and knowing eyes, his corpselike features crinkled with noble anguish. "Don't listen too much to your parents," his aunt said when he looked up from the cover. "They love you, but they're fearful people. They're afraid of what's inside their own heads. They're terrified of wandering away too far from the thoughts other people think."

He flipped through the gilt-edged pages. He thanked her.

His aunt had patted the back of his head, staring into his face. "When you get older, we will become very good friends," she said.

But this had not come to pass. His aunt and his parents drifted from one another, Helena spending less and less time in New Orleans, and his parents becoming more devout, more suspicious of his aunt and her books. All of those tales with adolescents holding séances in balmy attics and children befriending ancient crows. "The world's dark enough," his mother told him. "I don't know why my sister feels this need to make it darker."

By the time he was twelve, she had vanished from their lives.

Roland suspected those early years had counted, however. He bought his aunt's novels from a used bookstore on Baronne Street. *The Ashen Ones. Crow Eye. The House Without Walls.* He hid them under his bed. Read them as his parents slept. At times her stories were so close to the tales he wove in his own imagination that he almost suspected his aunt had written those novels for him. As if, somehow, she knew the workings of his own mind.

There was a link between them. Similar music played in their heads. A crackling record full of steep pauses.

Years later, when he received the phone call from a lawyer in Caleb soon after Helena's death, he was not entirely surprised.

"I've got some awful good news for you," the lawyer said, her voice tinged with a Cajun accent. She explained how Helena had left him her small fortune, an amount that would allow him, he realized, to live the rest of his days without work so long as kept to the austere lifestyle he had grown accustomed to over the last decades, working at a bookstore. She had also left him her house and property.

For a night, he wrestled with the question of what to do with that estate: sell it, or live in it. Not many ties kept him in New Orleans. His parents were dead, and he had few friends. And the idea of living out in the woods, alone, had a deep-rooted appeal.

His mother had frequently described his aunt as a hermit. He was sure he followed her in this trait, too, even if he had always dwelled in the city.

The afternoon he signed the papers at the lawyer's office, he drove over to the house, a place he had been to only once, when he was six or seven. As he rode up the curved gravel drive, he could tell his aunt Helena had not exactly kept the grounds neat: massive explosions of shrubbery encircled the brick building like a twiggy wreath, mushrooms sprouted from a few windowsills, and a long crack ran down the frosted glass of the front door.

Still, the fact this property had been his enigmatic aunt's, and now belonged to him, remained enthralling. He stepped inside the house, breathed in the air that still smelled of his aunt's body -- she had been discovered at least a week after her demise—and stared at the golden afternoon light touching the walls.

"I'm home, aunt Helena," he called out. "I'm here now."

Because Elizabeth was coming over, he vacuumed, and he swept the kitchen floor.

Never a big eater, he decided to have a cup of coffee for lunch.

As he drank, standing in the living room and thinking over the past few days, he glanced over at the wall facing east, and froze.

He closed his eyes, opened them again. What he saw remained the same. The windowless wall with its tur-quoise paint appeared slightly transparent, as if it were made from thick and clouded stained glass.

He swore he could make out the shape of the pecan tree that stood not far from the wall. The fat trunk, the upward jutting branches: the hell if he couldn't see it (just barely, yes, but absolutely visible) through the goddamn wall. His hand started to shake. The cup fell from his grasp, landing on the white shag carpet.

He walked over to the wall, staring through it at the tree.

A bird flew by, a dark speck darting through the yard.

Roland raised his quivering hand and brought his fingers to the wall, but he did not touch it. Just as he thought he felt a breath of air slip past through the wall, a suggestion of breeze touching his fingertips, he heard his phone buzz.

Elizabeth sending a text, telling him she would visit soon. She was headed out now.

He texted back, *This house has a mind of its fucking own.*

To which she replied, *Some houses can't help it.*

Then, seconds later, she wrote, *Seriously: You OK?*

Was he? If she saw what he saw, if she stood in front of the wall and could make out the tree standing beyond it, would he be happy to realize this craziness was not in his mind, but out there, in the world itself? Or would her confirmation make this that much worse? What was better: for your mind to unravel, or for reality to thread apart?

He placed the phone down on the coffee table, not having answered her last text, and turned to the wall again. He noticed something else: there, at the root of the tree. A clump. A big clump that appeared to be a blanket with a pile of burnt logs on top.

Roland marched through the screen door and down the stone steps leading into the weedy, fern-bordered garden, his eyes locked on the blanket and its load. The closer he came the less the pile looked like logs. They reshaped themselves with every step he took.

Limbs. That was what he thought they were.

Thick animal limbs with an ashen substance covering over them.

The blanket he had never seen before. A crimson blanket dotted with lilies. He stood in bewilderment next to the pile, the hot September sun glowing hard against his lank hair, pressing through the thin cloth of his t-shirt. The air smelled of grilled meat. But he scanned the area around the garden and saw no fire burning, no smoke.

A few feet away laid a long stick. He bent and grabbed it and held it out and poked into the pile of whatever it was on the blanket. One of the thicker objects rolled down, stopping at the toe of his boot, and he saw a human hand jutting from the end of it.

The shock knocked him back a step. He had to balance

his weight on the stick as if it were a cane to keep from tripping over. He inhaled and tried to gather strength. He looked again. The palm was covered in ash, but the tips of the fingers showed through the grey. He pressed the tip of the stick against the wrist, then the palm.

The fingers closed over the end of the stick like teeth biting down.

Then the day turned dark around him, and quiet. As if he were falling through the ground into a cool, deep hole.

As his vision cleared, and the sounds of the world returned, he realized he had made his way inside. Into the kitchen. He was perched on the edge of a kitchen chair, head in his hands. He raised up, brushing the wetness from his cheeks with the back of his hand. His eyes glided up to the clock near the sink but no matter how many times he tried to read the hands, he couldn't. They were written in a different language now.

Outside, a car door slammed.

Roland met Elizabeth on the porch, his right leg shaking so hard it was difficult to remain upright. He said, "I'm glad you're here. I don't know if I can take much more."

She stared into his face. She squeezed his shoulder. "Roland, just calm down."

"There's something in the back yard you need to see."

"Calm down first, all right? Just take some deep breaths." She took him by the arm and led him inside the house. She drew him over to the couch, gently pushed him down. Then she returned to the door. Closed it with her eyes locked on his face. Examining him as if he were pages from an almost illegible book. "Calm down," she repeated, softly.

"I can't. Not until I know if you see it too."

"See what?"

"The thing I found in the backyard."

She went over to the French door that looked out into the garden. "That pile of burnt up logs out there? Yeah. I see it, too."

He started to stand, but realized his legs were too weak, too watery. "You do? You see that goddamn arm out there?"

At first, she didn't answer. She continued looking out. The room was growing dim. He had not been able to read the kitchen clock, but it was clearly getting close to nightfall. "You see it," he repeated.

Several seconds passed before she said, "I do." She moved away from the window and crossed her arms. "Did you ever finish reading that book"?" she asked.

"Book? What do you mean?"

"*Regina Ignis*. You finish it yet?"

He hadn't picked it up in days: reading had become impossible recently. "I haven't. Why are you asking?"

"Didn't all this shit start the morning you read it?"

He nodded. He was interested in magic, but some splinter of doubt had always stayed within him. It was poetry. It wasn't science. "It's just a book," he said. "Coincidence."

"The Queen of Fire."

"Yes. I know. I Googled the title."

Elizabeth sat on the coffee table, in front of him, and placed her hands on his knees. "We met before, you and me. I can't believe we've been hanging out all this time, and you never figured that out."

He didn't say anything.

"When you were six. When you visited her at this house."

It came to him a little. A few scattered, muffled memories. Late fall and the sky brittle blue and him and a girl a few years older playing in the shallow creek that ran far behind this house, then the day winding down, the sky's light seeping from above them. Their hands and bare feet caked in cold mud, and the two of them threading their way through the tree trunks toward his aunt's house. And once there, the fight between his mother and Helena. Mother yelling about how she couldn't leave him for even a few hours with Helena without her kid coming back filthy, and not even wearing his jacket on such a cold day. His aunt responding in her dry, even tone, saying how there was nothing wrong with getting a little dirty, and only weak people worried about the cold.

Roland asked Elizabeth, "How come you never told me we met before?"

"I guess I was hoping you'd remember on your own."

"You knew Helena."

"Knew her very well. I was basically a street kid. My

parents were horrible people. They were too busy hating each other to ever give a shit about me." She took his arm. She squeezed his wrist. "You aunt took me in. She let me live here, on her land, in her house. I'd sleep on couches, or in the woods when it was hot out."

She leaned forward, as if to tell him a secret. "Let's go outside. Now that you've calmed down, let's take a look and figure out where we stand."

He watched her rise, and he stood next to her, his bones feeling fragile in his body and his chest pumping with blood. "You should have told me," he said as they crossed the threshold.

"Maybe. But I never lied to you either."

His right leg began to tremble as they neared the arm. He picked up the stick he'd dropped earlier and leaned on it to take some weight off. Elizabeth squatted down next to the hand on the ground, and brought her own hand over it. As she lowered her fingers, the fingers on the ground moved slightly.

Then they were touching: fingertips to fingertips. There was an odd intimacy to it, as if Elizabeth knew the owner of the hand, and was welcoming it back home.

Next, she dabbed her fingers in the dense ash within the palm of the hand. She stood and drew a line of ash from her forehead down to the tip of her nose.

As he watched, Roland realized he smelled wood smoke and grilling meat again. Despite the fear he felt in his joints, he was suddenly incredibly hungry. He imagined himself crouched on the balls of his feet, devouring a smoky leg of lamb, the juices dripping from his jaw.

She brought her hands over his face. He closed his eyes.

He felt her finger draw a line from his forehead to the tip of his nose.

She said, "The dead, they're always calling us, drawing us out into the great outdoors. And the walls we call home fade and fade and fade."

They went over to the blanket. When Elizabeth lifted one ash-wrapped limb and threw it several feet away, Roland nodded to himself and did the same, and soon the two of them were working steadily through the pile, their hair and clothes darkening with the grey powder. The lower they went, the warmer the limbs became. At the bottom was a ball of ash: a ball with ragged red hair stuck to the back. Elizabeth lifted it up, holding it out to Roland.

"She saw herself in you. And you know you saw yourself in her. When you look in the mirror, don't you see a little speck of her in your eyes?"

He brushed some of the ash from the grim-looking object Elizabeth held. The powder was surprisingly hot, as if from a just extinguished fire, and soon he felt lips, human lips, and he brushed his thumb across them, exposing the mouth.

He remembered opening the package, his aunt next to him, rain pinging the window of his boyhood room.

"Try the eyes," Elizabeth said.

And he did. Removing the ash with his thumbs. Brushing the sooty substance from the eyelids and eyebrows.

They opened as if from a long nap. No gaze had ever seemed so familiar.

Except he wasn't looking at the head Elizabeth was holding. He was staring from that head outwards, at himself.

From Elizabeth's grip he watched as his own mouth opened, his lips parting. "We're home, Roland," his aunt said through his voice. "We're together in the same book now."

She was right. He could feel himself standing, the heat of the sun brushing his back. And he could see himself from his aunt's eyes. He inhabited two places, just as she did. He murmured from his aunt's mouth, "Inside out."

He could feel Elizabeth's fingernails brushing through the matted hair of the scalp. She brought her lips to the ear and said, "The walls, you can see right through them, can't you?"

His gaze wondered to the house, which was burning now, tremendous tongues of fire licking at the windows as if wanting out. Somehow, he knew it had been burning for a very long time. Elizabeth held the head higher, so he could fully see the beauty of the flames.

The Whisperer
L.A. Story

June, 1945
Henderson Plantation
Calvary, Tennessee

"What's this? Some of that voodoo shit?" Mr. Henderson demanded.

Raven had been using the wash basin to clean herself after two hours in bed with him. She turned, holding the thin rag she used as a wash cloth. Her dark eyes widened when she saw he had opened the old wardrobe in the corner and pushed aside her few meager garments and a simple coat to find the tiny altar hidden in the back.

Her eyes moved from the altar to his face, which had darkened dangerously. He was a hard, violent man by nature. She could tell he wanted to be angry, wanted a reason to hurt her.

"Oh, no... No, Mr. Henderson, I promise it's not," she said. Still naked, she crossed the small bedroom to stand next to him. She reached into the wardrobe and touched a small knob on the bottom of the box that served as an altar. She pulled open a drawer and retrieved a small, porcelain figurine of the Blessed Virgin Mary and a set of rosary beads. She sat the figurine on top of the altar and laid the rosary in the brass bowl on top.

"See? It's a prayer altar," she said. "Christian."

She watched his face as she would the mercury level in a thermometer to gauge his mood. She felt only a small measure of relief when she saw that his normal color appeared to be returning. His blue eyes were still cold as he reached out and took her chin in a rough grip. He twisted her face to look at him. At six feet, she stood as tall as he was, but he was much broader and more heavily muscled. He studied her to catch any hint that a lie may be sneaking through her eyes. He was a terrifyingly shrewd man.

Seeing no evidence of deception, he let her go. She stifled

a sigh of relief, but there would be no true reprieve until he left her ramshackle little cottage.

He turned and took a few steps away to where he had hung his clothes on a knob at the foot of her old brass bed. Actually, it was *his* brass bed, she thought bitterly, his house and in a manner of speaking, she was his, too. Slavery may have been abolished a long time ago, but its cousin was still alive and well in the life of a share cropper's family. He was the plantation boss and her family was among those who worked the land. Her whole family depended on her to remain in Mr. Henderson's good graces. Otherwise, he could evict them and revoke their claim and there was no way that she would let it happen.

This was their land. Henderson just didn't know it, yet.

She quietly moved back toward the wash basin.

"Don't," he snarled. "Don't wash me off."

She didn't say anything, but she put down the wash cloth she still had clutched in her fist and reached for her undergarments and her simple, faded shirtwaist dress. She finished dressing just as he tucked in his work shirt and pulled his suspenders up over his big shoulders. He walked around the bed and she quickly darted out of his way as he went to the wash basin. He used the crude lye soap and washed his hands and used some extra water to slick back his reddish blonde hair. He was almost handsome, but had features too cruel and just a bit too ruddy—particularly in extreme temperatures. It was what made his moods so easy to read.

"Would you like me to fix you somethin' to eat before you go back to work, Mr. Henderson?" she asked.

"Nah, I can get something up at the house. Your mama will have food ready for me," he said, stiffly. Now that his lust was slaked, he was formal, almost prim. She knew he hated that he wanted her. He was the white owner of the plantation. She was black and her family was his contracted tenants and employees, although Raven rarely worked the cotton fields anymore. He kept her on as a domestic. He preferred to keep her close.

His sense of superiority was bred into him. As far as she knew, he didn't take any of the other female employees to bed. Just her. And, it pissed him off. He didn't want to want her as badly as he did. Part of him hated her, maybe even blamed her for his lust and obsession.

He grabbed up his wide-brimmed hat and gave her a nod. She shut the door behind him and did not breathe until she heard his heavy work boots leave her tiny porch. She sagged against the door for a moment before rushing to a small window adjacent to the front entrance. She lifted the burlap curtain and peeked out to see if anyone had been around to witness her shame—seeing the boss leaving her cottage after so long a visit.

There were similar little houses nearby, but thankfully no one else seemed to be around. It appeared everyone else was still out in the fields.

After a respectable amount of time, she put on her nylons and her clunky, functional shoes and headed up to the main house.

However, before she left her porch, she waved a hand in front of her door and murmured a protection spell. No one would enter her home without her there.

If they tried, they would be sorry.

Everyone in their camp knew it. It's why no one, except the boss, ever bothered her.

They knew Raven's family and feared them.

They knew better than to mess with witches.

Raven arrived at the main house through the kitchen door in the back. Her mother, Yvette, was putting a platter together, her popular five-hour stew, thick slices of homemade bread and a piece of chess pie for dessert. Raven didn't have to ask to know who the meal was for.

"Was it bad today?" her mother asked as she prepared the tray to take to the boss, probably in his office, where he usually took his midday meal.

Raven went to the peg where the aprons were kept and worked to tie one around her waist.

"It's always bad. It's humiliatin', but he didn't hit me today, so I s'pose that's good," she murmured.

"Does he know? Could he tell?"

Raven felt a chill go through her. "Not yet."

Yvette hefted the tray. She usually kept her dark eyes impassive, but Raven caught a glimmer of fear. The emotion was not for herself, but for Raven.

"He won't be happy about the baby," she said.

Raven shook her head. "No, Mama, he won't be happy about it at all."

There was a soft gasp from the doorway between the kitchen and the dining room.

The boss' wife, Jean Henderson, stood there. Her blue eyes were wide with shock.

"What baby?" she asked.

Yvette and Raven froze.

"What *baby*?" Her repeated question was hissed out in a vicious whisper.

Yvette looked at Raven. Fear blatant in her eyes. In many ways, Jean Henderson was scarier than her husband. Everyone knew that Mrs. Henderson was barren. The couple had been married for years and produced no children. She was notoriously sensitive about the subject.

"I'm expecting a baby, Mrs. Henderson," Raven answered, quietly. She kept her eyes downcast. She heard the sharp intake of breath and dreaded the question she knew would naturally follow.

"Oh? Who is the lucky father?"

Fear made Raven's mind go blank. Thankfully, her mother reacted quickly.

"Oh, he's the son of one of my oldest friends," she said. "He was visiting a while back and took a liking to Raven."

Yvette didn't look convinced. "Really? What's his name?"

"You don't know him. His family is from Mississippi," Yvette hedged.

"I might know him if he has a connection around these parts," said Jean.

"His name is Robert … Robert Johnson," she said.

Raven would have laughed if the situation hadn't been so terrifying.

The boss' wife seemed to consider it for a moment.

"I guess I'm not familiar with him," she finally admitted, although she didn't seem entirely convinced.

"He's a musician," Yvette said, lying as smooth as her famous butter cream frosting. "I'm 'fraid he left my girl high and dry."

"Oh, that's terrible." Jean Henderson's expression did not bear the weight of her vocal sympathy.

"We all have our burdens to bear," Yvette said, with a sigh. She lifted a food-laden tray. "Now, if you will excuse me, I have to get lunch to Mr. Henderson before it gets cold."

The lady of the house gave Yvette a curt nod and stepped out of the way. She gave Raven a long, cold and calculating look before she turned on her sensible heel and stomped away. She was so loud that Raven could track her progress through the house, up the stairs, and all the way to her bedroom.

It was only after the bedroom door slammed shut that Raven breathed a sigh of relief.

She gathered her basket of cleaning supplies and got started with her day's work, careful to monitor Mrs. Henderson's whereabouts at all times so as to avoid her.

After the evening supper dishes were done, Raven made the weary walk with her mother toward their row cottages. Her father and two brothers were home and getting washed up as Yvette heated the meal she had made for her family that morning—a batch of the same savory stew she made for the Henderson's, only made with less meat—and a pan of her sour cream cornbread.

In the middle of the meal, Yvette announced to the rest of the family, "Mrs. Henderson knows Raven is pregnant."

Saul Miller, her father, and her two brothers, Samuel and Isaac, were rendered mute and motionless. All eyes turned to Raven.

Finally, after a long pause, Saul asked, "Do she know who the daddy is?"

Yvette shook her head and told them what she had said.

Saul snorted. "Leave it to you to bring Johnson into this. You love his music."

"I can't believe you said that, Mama," said Isaac, laughing and slapping the table.

Samuel, always the more serious of Raven's two brothers, gazed at Raven as the others had a good laugh at

Yvette's quick thinking. He focused an unnerving gaze at his older sister. "We need to do a blessing spell over your baby before you leave here tonight. For protection."

They all quieted. Samuel knew things. He was not as talented as his mother or Raven at casting, but he could work a passable protection spell. Samuel's real talent came in his divination abilities.

"What do you know? What have you Seen?" Raven asked. She couldn't quite keep the tremor from her voice.

"Not clear, yet." He began to dig into his stew again. He spoke between bites. "All I can see is danger."

"If Mr. Henderson finds out the baby is his and he's mad about it... Could he kick us off our claim?" Isaac asked. He turned fearful eyes to Saul.

Their father's jaw clenched and relaxed as he fought back his anger at the suggestion. After a moment of consideration, he shook his head. "Nah, I don't think he would do that 'cause we still owe at the company store and our yield is always better at harvest."

"What do you think he'd do then?" Yvette whispered, as though Henderson were listening right outside the door.

"I think he'd make our lives mo' miserable than he already do. I think he would find mo' ways to make us beholden' to him," Saul said. His dark eyes were grim. "The only reason he ain't done that is 'cause of Raven. He wanted her and he makes things a touch better 'cause he has her now and again."

Raven looked down into her soup bowl, shame squelching her appetite. Her father had never before openly discussed what Henderson did with her. She knew her father was aware of it, but hearing him say it was unbearable.

Henderson had threatened to kick them out if she didn't spend time with him. He offered to lower their rent a bit and provide them with a little more credit at the company store between harvests. She did whatever she had to do to make their lives less hard.

They all quietly finished their meal.

After the dishes were done, her mother pulled out a brass bowl, handmade candles, oils, herbs and other items for a protection and blessing spell. Saul didn't care for the working of magick. He was not a practitioner, but he knew what Yvette could do and Raven and Samuel had inherited their abilities from her. Saul and Isaac usually just went for a walk while the witches did their work.

Yvette, Raven, and Samuel washed up and each slipped into their robes, each garment was simply made. They stood barefoot around the kitchen table, which had been converted from an ordinary, battered old wood table, to a ceremonial altar.

Yvette added herbs and oils to the bowl as she chanted, "I toss these offerings into the bowl for the riches of blessings to be made whole. Let it represent Earth within this spell, for Raven's child to remain well."

Outside the small home, the wind had kicked up enough to rattle the homemade wooden chimes hanging from the porch awning.

Samuel added a hawk feather and two drops of water. He waved his hands over the bowl, hands so dark and graceful that Raven considered it an insult that they carried the calluses and scars of a common laborer.

"Please accept my offering to be wind and rain, to capture power in this spell to gain," Samuel chanted. "Keep this babe free from all worry and bother. Keep it away from the wrath of its father."

The wind began to blow in stronger gusts. The screen door suddenly was blown open to slam against the wall outside.

Raven lit a match and dropped it into the bowl. A flame leapt high and began to consume the other ingredients.

"And now I add fire with the heat to affect, a spell with the enduring strength to protect," Raven felt the additional power humming through her as she always did when working magick with her mother and brother. "I call on the spirit of Hadler's Wood, to protect my baby as only it could."

She stared into the flames but she felt the shocked glances from her mother and brother. No one called on the thing that inhabited the neighboring woods. No one. Ever.

Outside the wind began to moan and blow hard enough the cause the cottage's walls to shiver.

They joined hands around the flame and chanted together, "Blessing, well being and protection come, so as we will it, so let it be done."

The flame flared high. The wind howled and then the fire died as suddenly as it flared and the night went completely silent.

Raven felt a shiver go through her and knew the spell was solid. She breathed a sigh of relief until her brother rounded on her.

"Why did you do that? Why not just work a spell the way we're supposed to? Why would you call on a strange spirit? Do you have any idea what you've done?"

Raven straightened her spine. "I'm not a child. There is power in whatever lives in Hadler's Woods and I'm going to do whatever I have to."

"Yes, but Raven ... at what cost? It's never that easy, baby," Yvette said. Her dark eyes were frightened. "There's always price when you call on that kind of apparition."

With more courage that she actually felt, Raven said, "Then I will pay it."

Raven left her parents' home shortly afterward. Dawn always came much too soon and the next day was laundry and linens, which would take nearly all their time. The day after was floors and rugs and the list never ended. At least the Henderson's large main house had electricity and indoor plumbing, although "the help" was never allowed to use it.

With the growing inconvenience of her pregnancy, Raven found that she tired a little more easily and her trips to the outhouse were more frequent. She allowed her hand to slide down to the place on her lower abdomen between her navel and the top of her mons—the place where her child rested and grew. That was how she thought of the tiny being—*her* child. Family was precious, no matter where they came from. Her family believed that and had raised her to believe it herself. It was hard-wired.

Now, as she walked the two rows over to her own tiny cottage, she took a moment to enjoy the scents of an aging summer. Harvest time would soon be in its prime. She could smell it on the humid breeze. The wind had died after their spell casting, but now seemed to be picking up again as she carefully made her way along the cottage rows. Although faint, flickering lights could be seen within a few homes, she knew most folks had already gone to bed for the night. Sharecropping was grueling work with long hours. The hardest workers had the best chance for yields high enough to make a profit for more than just the landowner. Mr. Henderson profited well off the sweat of the sharecroppers who worked his land.

Raven made her way through the darkness and was almost to her tiny front porch, when she heard a voice whisper her name.

Raven. Raven.

She gasped softly and glanced around but there were only cottages in the faint moonlight and deeper shadows within shadows. She stepped up onto her porch and listened carefully. When she didn't hear anything else, she disengaged the wards she put in place to guard her home and she went inside. She barred her door once she was safely within.

It was dark inside the cottage. She cursed the Henderson's for not wiring the cottages for electricity. She didn't risk fire by leaving a kerosene lamp burning and it was too hot for the fireplace this time of year; thus, her one room home was an assembly of familiar shadows, but now something was different.

She sensed she was not alone.

Raven was a witch of considerable power, and never had been the type one would consider fragile, but the presence she sensed within her home was far beyond anything she'd ever experienced.

In the dark, she felt her way toward the tiny kitchen area opposite her bed and found her matches on a small shelf. An icy touch ran along the back of her neck and she shivered in spite of the hot summer evening. She found her hurricane lamp and removed the glass chimney from the burner prongs and she struck a match and touched it to the wick. It caught after a moment and she turned the knob to adjust the light and then put the chimney back in place.

The soft glow of the lamp added enough light to the room to give her some comfort and she could pretend she didn't feel something powerful following her every move around the cottage.

She placed the lamp in the center of her small dining table and crossed the room to light the lamp which sat on the table next to her bed. As she leaned over to light the wick, she heard the distinctive sound of footsteps across the room, near where she had been moments before.

Raven froze with the lit match burning down to her fingers. She shook it out to keep from getting burned.

"Who's there?" she whispered.

When no answer came, she mentally chided herself for being foolish. Her cottage was tiny. If there were someone in the room with her, there was no place for them to hide.

A thump by her wardrobe made her jump. For several moments, she sat, tense and waiting, but slowly relaxed when nothing further happened. She changed her mind about lighting the lamp by her bed. Instead, she went to her wardrobe and pulled out a thin sleeping shift. She washed up and dressed for bed. She snuffed the lamp, crawled into bed, and drifted into restless sleep where she dreamed she was in the woods, running from unseen terrors while clutching a crying baby to her bosom.

She awoke in tears, surrounded by the ghostly fading sounds of a newborn baby's cry.

Over the next few weeks, a disturbing pattern developed at the main house. Obviously resentful of Raven's pregnancy, Jean Henderson set out to make Raven's life more miserable than it already was. She tested Raven's resolve to remain employed by making the work more difficult and she tried to humiliate Raven at every opportunity.

Often the tricks the boss' wife pulled were petty and inconvenient such as spilling dried beans on the floor of the kitchen and letting Raven know that she was fired if every single scattered bean wasn't found.

The vicious tricks didn't stop there.

Mrs. Henderson poured flour on one of the largest rugs in the house and then doused it with water. It took hours and hours of scrubbing on her hands and knees to clean up that mess. Mrs. Henderson took every opportunity to spill liquids and make messes that made Raven's life hard.

The worst, and the most disgusting and disturbing, passive-aggressive attack took place in the small water closet downstairs. The Hendersons were proud of their indoor plumbing. They had a water closet upstairs near the master bedroom as well.

Raven cleaned and sanitized these "indoor outhouses" each day. However, when she reached the downstairs water closet, she knew something was wrong before she even opened the door. First, the door was normally only closed when it was occupied. Raven came upon the water closet when the door was closed but there was no one in the tiny room. Second, she could smell the room before she even opened the door.

She knocked several times to make sure the room wasn't being used. Finally, she opened the door and was nearly knocked over by the stench of human waste. She fumbled in the dark for the pull string that would turn on the overhead light.

When the light came on Raven stumbled backward and was almost fell as she slipped on the feces that had been spread all over the floor. She covered her mouth and barely kept from falling. She let out a scream and then stumbled out of the room as she fought the urge to vomit.

Yvette came running when she heard Raven's scream. She came up short with a gasp as she and Raven both stared into the room with horrified eyes.

The sophisticated pot where a person did one's necessary business of elimination was covered in feces. The seat, the water tank high above, the handle, the walls, the floor ... the room had literally been painted with it.

"Mama, what kind of human being does this?" Raven gasped. Tears filled her eyes. She couldn't help it. The sheer shock of it and the contemplation of having to clean it was so overwhelming that she couldn't mask her emotions.

"A human being that's got something very, very wrong with them," her mother whispered with a quick glance over her shoulder. They never knew when Jean Henderson would be upon them. She could move with an eerie stealth when she wanted.

Raven shuddered.

Slowly, Raven gathered several buckets of water and cleaning materials. She put on a heavy apron to protect her dress as much as she could. The mess took her the better part of a day—at least five hours. She gagged off and on the whole time, but was proud of herself for not losing her breakfast.

That night, her mother prepared Raven a hot bath in their larger cottage. Her father and brothers made themselves scarce as Yvette helped Raven scrub the filth from her body and they took extra care to clean her shoes and clothes.

Even freshly bathed, Raven didn't feel clean. She went home after dark and slipped into her night clothes. She had fallen into an exhausted sleep, but was roused into an abrupt wakefulness by a midnight knock at the door.

It had been weeks, but she knew Mr. Henderson had held back as long as he could. This was the way it always had been. He would come to her and take her again and again until his lust was sated. He always waited until his need for her was too much for him to bear any longer. He always came to her desperate and aggressive, such was his obsession.

She came to the door and pressed her ear to the heavy wood. "Who is it?"

"Who do you think? Now let me in," he hissed. He kept his voice low because he didn't want anyone in the neighboring cottages to witness him entering her home.

She took the bar off the door and slowly opened it a crack, but he pushed his way in and quickly closed and barred it.

When that was done he turned and pulled the suspenders off his shoulders and untucked his shirt as he approached her.

"Take that gown off," he ordered as he finished undressing.

She quietly obeyed.

He grabbed for her roughly and pushed her down onto the bed. He looked half crazy and she hid her fear. If he sensed fear, it made it worse. He was on her before she could even gasp her shock. He seemed more desperate than usual.

It was a while later, after he had taken was he needed from her, he sat up and placed his hand on her lower abdomen, which was now obviously swelling with her growing child.

"So, it's true then. You're pregnant," he said, with something akin to wonder in his voice. It was not an emotion she expected, but it was not a healthy sort of wonder... he stared at her pregnant belly with a frightening intensity.

"Yes, it's true," she whispered.

"Mrs. Henderson told me about it... she also told me what your mama said about who the father was... that's not true though. Is it?" His eyes finally moved up to meet hers. He grabbed her chin and leaned over her. "Tell me the truth. Am I the father?"

She swallowed. She didn't know which answer would keep her and her baby safe. She decided the truth might be the best option. "Yes. You're the father."

He let go of her chin and simply stared at her.

"Does anyone else know?"

"Just my family. You know they won't tell anyone," she said.

He barked out a harsh laugh. "Yeah, I know they better not tell anyone."

He shook his head and made a sound of something like disgust. "I can't conceive with my lawful wife, but I managed to get you knocked up. The help. It's a kick in the pants."

She should have been humiliated by his derisive tone, but she expected his attitude. There was no surprise there. Her only shame was that he was the father—this mean and manipulative employer. It nothing she would have wanted. She only gave herself to him to help her family.

"Are you going to send us away?" she asked.

He got up and walked around the bed to the water basin where he washed up. He spoke as he washed. "Nah... I don't think so. As long as no one else knows, I don't see a reason to end our arrangement and lose my best sharecroppers."

She suppressed her sigh of relief. There were other farms to which her family could go and find employment, but they had personal reasons for staying on the Henderson Plantation. Her father was convinced it was their land based on a very old promise back in the days when the slaves were freed. It was generations back, but the old plantation owner had promised the farm to Raven's family. Of course, things hadn't worked out. They were robbed of their inheritance when the promise was not recognized by the powers that be. Instead, they were sharecroppers on the same land they were promised.

Her father said times were changing and one day they would own the land on which they lived and worked. Because of that, they were determined to remain right where they were.

Because of that promise, Raven also remained. When Mr. Henderson had approached her with a proposition, she agreed to it because it helped her family, even if he was mean and rough. He was simply a means to an end.

Presently, he was dressed and she rose from the bed and slipped on a robe to see him out. He unbarred the door and stepped outside and froze where he stood on the porch. His eyes were fixed on a spot down at the bottom of the porch steps. From inside the cottage, Raven couldn't see what he was looking at, but she heard an angry screech and her blood went cold.

"You baaaasssstarddddd… you damn perverted bastard!!" Jean Henderson screamed from the bottom of the steps.

Raven started to tremble. She moved forward to see the boss's wife standing in the bare patch at the foot of her porch steps. She was in her gown and her mousy brownish hair was a mess as if she had been clutching at it. The morning sun was just beginning to come up and the sunlight illuminated his wife's scrawny body through the thin gown. It was positively unseemly for her to be out here looking like this.

"Are you crazy, woman? Get back up to the house and get your clothes on! NOW!" Henderson bellowed.

Jean Henderson flinched but then turned her eyes toward Raven and a look of such hatred twisted her featured that Raven was nearly tempted to withdraw back into the cottage, but she was tired of hiding.

Mrs. Henderson hissed, "You! You lying bitch!! I knew it! I *knew* it!"

Other employees were slowing emerging from their cottages to witness the drama and Raven's humiliation.

Jean Henderson pointed a bony finger in Raven's direction and she turned her poisonous glare back to her husband. "She can no longer work in the main house! I won't tolerate it!"

Mr. Henderson's coloring was slowing turning a deeper red. Raven backed into the cottage with a simple sense of self-preservation. She knew he was about to lose his temper. Jean Henderson was too furious and crazed to realize she was in danger.

He stomped down the steps and grabbed his wife by the arm. "You don't *ever* get to speak that way to me, woman!"

He glanced back at Raven, who peeked through an adjacent window as he physically dragged his wife away from the workers' cottages. His expression was thunderous. Jean Henderson screeched, screamed and scratched at him like an angry cat all the way up to the main house.

Raven shut her door and barred it. She went over to her bed, sat down, buried her face in her hands and cried for the fate of her family and her unborn child.

Mr. Henderson came back hours later and announced that Raven and her family could stay but Raven would have to start working in the fields again. His tone was cold, but his eyes blazed as he raked them over her body. She worried he would take her again, but he abruptly turned on his heel and left without another word.

It was brutally hard work, but she'd done it before being taken into the main house. She would survive.

She tended the vegetable garden while her father and brothers worked the cotton fields. The vegetable garden was the closest to the edge of Hadler's Woods. She heard her name on the wind more than once. She was certain she was going as mad as Jean Henderson. The Whisperer was seeking her attention.

Raven... Raven... come to me and I can give you what

you want.

Raven decided voice of The Whisperer of Hadler's Woods was decidedly feminine.

"I am not ready. I can do this by myself. I don't need to come to you," she whispered back and hoped no one else was around to hear her.

You will come... soon enough. The Whisperer replied. *When you come, make sure you come to me in the daylight. Do not ever approach Hadler's Woods at night. There are things here that would do you harm before I could reach you.*

Strange things were known to happen in Hadler's Woods at night. Raven knew better than to ever show up there after dark.

She shook her head. "You are not real. I'm hearing things."

Suit yourself, but remember ... you summoned me. I will be here when you decide you need me. We can help each other, Raven. Don't wait until it's too late.

That statement chilled Raven's blood like an early frost.

The harvest couldn't come soon enough for Raven. She had grown quite large with child by the time everything was harvested. The next projects were the endless canning, dehydrating, and preserving vegetables, fruits, and salting and smoking meat for the winter.

Raven went into labor earlier than expected and it was a hard labor that lasted for hours, but when the time came, she pushed a daughter into the world and ten minutes later, she birthed another daughter.

She gazed at her twin girls—both so perfect—squalling and wriggling.

Her mother had helped her with the birth and worked blessing spells for healing and blessed lives, afterward.

Exhausted from the long labor, Raven took each babe to her breast in turn to nourish them and she said, "These are my precious jewels. They will be named Ruby and Pearl."

The next morning, Mr. Henderson came to Raven's cottage to see the babies.

Raven was uncomfortable having him near her children, but she tolerated his presence. Yvette and Samuel were with her, helping with the babies. Her brother was unusually good with children. Her father had been by earlier to dote on his granddaughters and had just left.

The boss gazed at his daughters with a strange light in his eyes. "As soon as you are able, you will bring them to the main house. They will be raised with us. You will be kept as a wet nurse for as long as is needed, of course."

"What?" Raven gasped and looked helplessly at her mother.

"Mr. Henderson," Yvette spoke up. "You can't just claim Raven's babies like that, Sir. Besides, what would you be wanting with two black children, anyway?"

He looked sharply at Yvette. "I'm their father and the plantation owner and your boss. I think I can do whatever the hell I want. Jean and I have been wanting babies for years. I think they will do just fine."

With one last look at the infants, and a smoldering glance at Raven, he turned and left.

A rage like nothing she had ever felt began to build within her.

She looked to her mother. "He's not taking my babies."

Yvette looked frightened and she lifted Ruby and cuddled the newborn to her chest. "I don't know what we'll do but we can always pack up and leave. We won't let him have them, Raven."

"We're not leaving!" Raven snapped as she struggled to get out of bed. "And, he's not getting my babies!"

"Raven! Get back in bed. You just gave birth less than a day ago. You're still weak," Yvette cried.

Raven threw on her robe. She knew what she had to do... and who she needed to see.

The Whisperer.

Samuel laid Pearl into a large basket that had been fashioned into a bassinet. He tried to stop his sister from leaving, but she raised her arms and summoned wind. It was one of the few things she could do without casting a spell.

"Don't make me do you harm, Samuel," she cried as the wind outside plucked at the open door, making it sway gently.

He wisely backed off and she fled barefoot to Hadler's Woods while it was still daylight.

It was late October and the ground was cold and branches and thorns tore at Raven's feet and it wasn't long before she was shivering within her thin robe and gown.

She screamed as she ran. "I am here! Where are you? You said you would help!"

Her bloodied feet pounded the ground as she moved as quickly as she could even though she had no idea where she was going.

Finally, exhausted and cold, she dropped to her knees. She could feel something wet and sticky dripping down her thighs and she knew she was bleeding from her womb, which was still raw from birthing her daughters.

As she listened to the sound of her own ragged breathing, she realized that her breathing was all she could hear. There was a sudden and unnatural stillness to the woods around her.

A familiar touch, icy and invisible, ran up her back. Raven was no longer alone.

What would you give up to obtain a guarantee for your daughters' safety? Hm? The Whispered asked.

Raven didn't hesitate. "Anything!"

I need a corporeal form, Raven. Would you give up your life for Ruby and Pearl? I am a powerful witch, child. I am far older and more powerful than you can imagine, but I need a body to do the work I was meant to do in this world. If you do this for me, then I will vow to always watch over your children.

She didn't want to die, but she knew her family could take care of the girls. She sensed that this entity was sincere. She could *feel* it.

"What about the rest of my family?"

Oh, they will get what they were promised. I have watched over your family since long before you were born, my dear. I knew eventually your clan would produce a witch strong enough to hold me. You are that witch, Raven. I know what was taken from your family and it will be restored. All you have to do is say, 'yes.' You will get peace. I will get a body. Your daughters will be protected and your family will prosper. It is a noble sacrifice, is it not?

Raven nodded mutely.

The whole world seemed to hold its breath while she made a choice.

Finally, she said, "I accept your offer. What do I have to do?"

Immediately, she felt a gentle pressure push her until she was lying on her back. The cold ground caused her to shiver harder and her teeth began to chatter.

Take deep breaths in and out. It takes a lot of magick to make this work. The elements around us will be affected by this kind of power. Don't be afraid, Raven. Just keep taking slow, deep breaths... in and out... I will do the rest.

With tears streaming back from her eyes, Raven did as she was instructed. In her mind, she said good-bye to her babies, her mother and father, and her brothers.

The wind picked up and clouds blotted out the sun. The wind gusted stronger and it plucked at her clothes and her hair and stirred up debris around her. She could feel the power circling her. Lightning flashed and thunder rolled in an ominous growl. Raven closed her eyes and concentrated on calming her pounding heart. Was it truly possible to be scared to death?

Suddenly, she felt something move over her prone body.

Deep breath in, Raven, said The Whisperer.

As Raven took a deep breath, she felt something strange. It was as if she had inhaled a drug. She felt dizzy and disoriented as warmth began to spread through her veins. The warmth increased until she felt as if she were boiling from the inside out and she let out a terrible scream.

Deep breath out, Raven... and let go... just let go. Now The Whisperer's voice was coming from inside her head.

Raven didn't know how. It was like she had forgotten how to breathe. Suddenly, she felt the breath leave her body and she suddenly realized what she needed to do.

Let go, the Whisperer had said. Raven now knew that was not the entity's true name. Raven also knew she would keep her word.

Raven surrendered her mortality and let go.

As her sense of the world began to fade, she knew everything was going to be all right.

For several long moments after Raven's spirit departed, her body was still in death.

Finally, the body jerked and her eyes flew open as another being looked out at the world. She drew a deep breath and let out a triumphant scream that scattered birds into the sky, which was rapidly clearing of the storm.

Yvette Miller looked up and let out a relieved cry as Raven appeared in the doorway just after dark.

She rose from her chair and laid a baby down into the nearest empty basket.

"Raven, you had us so scared!" she said as she approached her daughter. Raven's gown was filthy and there was blood running down her legs. "Darlin', let me get you cleaned up and back in bed. You're bleeding and you're still weak from giving birth to those sweet girls."

Raven looked at her with a strange expression, but said nothing.

Yvette took her daughter's hand, noting it wasn't as cold to the touch as she would have expected after being outside for so long. Raven allowed her to draw her into the cottage.

Yvette nodded toward a neighbor, Sarah, who was nursing Pearl.

"The babies were hungry, so Sarah volunteered to help feed them until you came back," Yvette explained.

Raven nodded, but said nothing.

Yvette felt a sliver of alarm. What was wrong with her girl?

Her daughter sat patiently on the side of the bed as Yvette heated water to prepare a bath. Raven allowed Yvette to help her bathe and change into clean, dry clothes, but she didn't speak until she was tucked beneath the covers.

"Yvette," she said. "You and Saul will raise Ruby and Pearl. I will be leaving here in the morning, but I won't be far away if you need me."

"What do you mean?" Yvette asked. Though she was confused, she felt a terrible unease begin to work its way up her spine. "Why would you leave your children? Your family?"

"I will watch over you all. It's what I promised her. Do you understand, Yvette?" Raven's eyes looked at her with an intensity and power that Yvette knew her daughter didn't possess. There was a sense of "otherness" about her.

"You're not Raven, are you?" she whispered. She glanced over at Sarah, who seemed absorbed in the child she was feeding.

"I will continue to use the name. You may call me 'Raven,' but I am your daughter in body only," the new Raven replied.

Yvette felt hot tears sliding down her face. "What have you done to my daughter?"

"It was her choice," the stranger replied, coldly.

A terrible dread filled her, along with a soul crushing sense of loss. "What happens now?"

"I will be leaving... you and Saul will raise the children, but do not despair," said the stranger. "By morning, all will be set right with your family."

"What do you mean?" Yvette whispered.

Raven pulled a hand out from beneath the blankets and snapped her fingers. Somewhere in the distance outside the cottage, there was a loud "boom" and the ground shook.

Yvette trembled.

"It has begun," the Raven/stranger said, with a terrible smile then she fell asleep.

The fire at the main house killed Mr. Henderson and his wife. It was said that the screen in front of one of the fireplaces was knocked over when a log rolled out and no one knew what happened until it was too late. The plantation was too rural for fire trucks to reach them in time and the entire house burned to the ground.

Mysteriously, documents appeared proving the Millers' claim to the 100 acre farm.

Over the years, there were no more reports of The Whisperer, but disappearances and strange events continued to surround Hadler's Woods, particularly after dark.

Yvette figured no one would ever know the whole truth of what happened after Raven ran into the woods when Mr. Henderson threatened to try and take her children.

Raven Miller became a recluse, living apart from her family, but she would come by on special occasions from time to time.

The family never knew when to expect the familiar stranger who never seemed to age.

Each generation just knew to keep a wary eye on Hadler's Woods and know that their mysterious guardian was always watching.

Tickle, tickle, burn, burn
Nicola Currie

Tickle, tickle, burn, burn, the spell is in the skin,
the flesh in which the elders bound me to keep the magic in.

Tickle, tickle, burn, burn, it starting to crackle and split,
these young fools think they're wise, doomed as the flames
were lit.

Tickle, tickle, burn, burn, the rumours were easy to start.
A few dead cows, then a few sick babes, who died and broke
their hearts.

Tickle, tickle, burn, burn, my scheme prospers without a
hitch.
It is an ancient truth now long forgot that fire births a witch.

Tickle, tickle, burn, burn, the flame is amusing and true.
It is the only warmth in a witch's heart and does her bidding,
too.

Tickle, tickle, burn, burn, my prison body crumbles and
blacks.
How good it feels to cast it off and take my powers back.

Tickle, tickle, burn, burn, my beloved flame has left me
cleansed
and cackling at the many thoughts of how I'll have revenge.

Tickle, tickle, burn, burn, some I will jinx and hex.
Others will face their own execution as I break their pretty
necks.

Tickle, tickle, burn, burn, it will be delightful to have my say,
to see them realise what is coming, to hear them screaming
wild as they

burn, burn, burn, burn.

They Called Them Sleeping Beauties

Terrie Leigh Relf

My three sisters were in stasis while we journeyed through darkest space, their silent breath clinging to viscous glass in the med bay, their once pretty faces bulging through winter vines that tightened and expanded as they grew. We sought another world, their father's realm, hoping the spell would at last be lifted, that my sisters would return to their former state—But alas, the coordinates we had didn't lead to *Arbora,* and so we continued to journey throughout the void for nearly a hundred years.

Was it sabotage? Or another one of our mother's wayward spells?

"Such sleeping beauties," the members of each medical team rotation would say as they made their rounds, and I would agree with a catch in my breath, so as to seem supportive. For beautiful they never were, or ever would become... Was it mother's spell that made my sisters appear beautiful to all who beheld them but us? Given her disgust at their appearance, Mother bid me watch over them.

I suppose the medical team meant well, that there was a part within each one of them that believed in the power of positive suggestion, and that no harm would come from it.

Placed in stasis since their birth, my sisters continued to grow, and some might say, evolve. I often wondered if they were aware of themselves, each other, and those beyond their transparent glass confines. Mother had barely survived their birth, much less this journey, and spent most of her days confined to quarters.

It was also left to me to ensure my sisters were safely returned to their father's realm. When at last *Arbora* revealed itself, we remained cautious. Even I refrained from my usual dire thoughts, attempting to console Mother, whose appearance seemed to say that she barely ate or drank, much less slept. Would being returned to their father truly break our mother's wayward spell? If not, then what were we to do, as my sisters' bodies continued to transform, threatening to breach their stasis chambers.

As we attained geosynchronous orbit above the planet, a series of images began to reel within my mind. Could I actually be capable of disconnecting their stasis tubes? Or were my sisters telepathic and begging me for release? They appeared to sleep peacefully as we descended into the great maw of their father's landing bay. Our mother remained aboard, while most of the crew accepted the invitation "to disembark, take refreshment, enjoy some fresh air after your long and arduous journey." Their father appeared to be a polite, perhaps decent, man. I studied his face, his physique, and wondered if Mother had cast a spell to ensure his eternal youth. When he asked after her, I said, "She hasn't been well," to which he responded, "Perhaps I shall venture aboard to visit her. It has been a long time since I've been within her presence."

At last, my sisters' stasis chambers were transferred into their father's facilities. His medical staff took over, disconnected the portable life support systems we provided, then hooked up their own. Their father, whose name was difficult to pronounce within our tongue, peered through the glass, his expression shifting like a cloying mist from desire to curiosity, to... could that be disgust?

The earlier images of someone disconnecting the stasis tubes returned. While Mother had told me countless times that I'd never be the witch she was, could I have gifts of which she was unaware? After all, she was the one who cast the spell for her daughters to radiate with beauty like the flowers in her opulent gardens... I was the ugly unpleasant one, or so she always reminded me during her fits of frustration and angst. I may well have had thorns, for she never showed me affection, much less embraced me as she supposedly longed to do with my younger sisters.

"Unplug the chambers," I called out. "Unplug them now!"

Their father nodded to the med team. Despite their arguing against it, the team obeyed his order. One after the other, each tube was released with an audible hiss.

"Should we open the chambers?" their father asked.

Even the med team turned toward me. I nodded, and it was done.

An interminable silence was followed by the sound of something writhing. What followed this, continues to be difficult to describe, even more difficult to fathom...

Released at last, my three sisters burgeoned from their confines, limbs and tendrils flailing as if reaching out for something to grasp. Despite her insistence that reuniting my sisters with their father had been her reason for living, it was then that I realized why Mother chose not to be present for this long-awaited event.

My sisters had indeed evolved... horrendously so. Within minutes of their release, bulbous protrusions emerged, dangling from their limbs. A mere moment later, each one popped to reveal a multi-hued flower that soon released a spray of golden spores.

Most of us covered our mouths and noses, coughing, as we exited the medical bay in haste. The lead doctor shouted, "Turn on the containment field!"

Not everyone left in time...

Before I turned away from my mother's former lover's face pressed against the glass, I knew that Mother's spell had not been wayward after all.

Granny's Tincture for Astral Travel Mishaps
Terrie Leigh Relf

If you lie in bed near every night,
your spirit absent at dawn's first light,
Granny's tincture will ease your plight,
as Granny knows, she has the sight.

Your spirit journeys, and just might,
be trapped within a land of blight,
since your body is unable to take flight,
it remains behind, but not for spite.

For Granny can the spell rewrite,
so you can return, if not outright.
Just grant her the undivided right
to prepare you for a unique parasite.

In time, the creature will hold tight,
and your transformation, albeit slight,
will return you to this plane contrite,
whether or not you chose this quite.

Be not petrified with fright,
as soon the cords will be smite
joining you to realms of delight...
Come here, girl! My good little wight.

The Salted Circle

Gregory L. Norris

Hypnotic jazz drifted out of the kitchen—Brubek. Between the tracks, the world seemed to hold its breath. Chef Paul Leander shuffled through the open space, not quite dancing as he prepared what Nora hoped would be a meal as exquisite as planned, as *dreamed.* The sough of the wind outside, blowing down from the mountains, waned, and pressure built around the Hillside Inn, making it difficult to breathe.

Nora moved from room to room, checking last minute details, her steps on the ancient hardwood floors exaggerated by the sudden absence of the wind, which had gusted angrily all night, through most of the morning, and into the fading gray overcast of New Year's Eve Day.

The Hillside sparkled against the day's moody palette, from the Jamaican blue of the Forget-Me-Not Room to the frosty reds of the Primrose Suite. She adjusted the pomegranate throw at the end of the yellow bedspread in the Buttercup Room, replaced the lemon-verbena liquid hand soap in the hallway bathroom with a fresh bottle, and then drew her button-down sweater tight against an unexpected shiver. The window in the bathroom showed hints of the white hillsides that surrounded the inn and a few hundred acres of woods, pasture, meandering country roads, the skating pond, and the occasional house, identified only by wisps of smoke from a chimney. But a row of platinum-colored icicles hung off the roof, obscuring much of the view. Thick, waxy icicles, the image was of monstrous teeth. A long row of jagged fangs, waiting to bite, to sip blood.

The jazz cut out. End of CD, she told herself. Chef Paul would switch over to a new one, and once again the pleasant music would drift out of the sound system. But the wait between sets stretched out and she wondered if his almost-dance steps had been stilled by the oppressive shroud that hung over the world. The wind, which had moaned in a disembodied voice all night and throughout the day, kept silent, as though afraid to speak.

Nora gazed out the bathroom window, toward the surrounding hills. The shiver took an encore, despite the heat from the log fire roaring downstairs in the Wild Aster Salon's hearth, in the inn's general gathering space. She glided toward the staircase, passing framed antique botanicals and new watercolors painted by some of Cottage Valley's most talented artists, a two-dimensional garden in full bloom in defiance of the brutal winter beyond. But a garden also standing rigid in anticipation, like so many of the day's elements.

Nora reached the bottom of the stairs. The music started up again as she rounded the Newell Post. Something light, cheery—Bossa Nova from Brazil. The luscious aroma of roasting garlic shattered the spell of paralysis hanging over the inn. Chef Paul hummed while chopping a bulb of fresh fennel.

"Yummy," she said.

The lone word emerged into that strange atmosphere sounding sluggish, a full octave deeper than Nora expected. Chef Paul turned, the smile on his attractive face heavy, crooked, as though the result of anesthesia. Bossa Nova played and chirped in the face of the shroud.

"Paul, can I ask you..." she started.

He chopped, tipped his chin up in invitation for her to complete the thought.

Nora waved both hands in dismissal. "Forget it."

"You're talking about that odd undercurrent of energy?"

"You feel it, too?"

"Maybe it's just nerves," Paul said. He broke focus. "Or it's Divina Cortland."

"The witch?" Nora said, punctuating the statement with a humorless chuckle.

"Witch, hag, *demon*—whatever she was, the people in this valley still sleep with one eye open, over a hundred years after she vanished into those hills."

Chef Paul aimed the blade of his knife toward the vast wall of windows in the Wild Aster Salon that faced the snowy slopes.

The place was a mess the first time she toured the old farmhouse. Six months after their initial greeting on a bright June morning, the inn had transformed, incorporating the best of the new with the finest of the old. Hand-blown cranberry glass pendant lights cast a warm glow on the antique floor of the kitchen. A new network of built-in bookcases in the Wild Aster Salon had the best of used books, beloved classics bought at local yard sales and secondhand shops, like the floral artwork on walls and easels. The door to the Queen Anne's Lace Room wasn't plumb, required a jamb to keep it open, but the heating system, metal roof, and well were top-of-the-line recent additions.

The sagging, sad farmhouse had been transformed; the inn radiated elegance, comfort. Not simply a place to stay, Nora had sold it as a destination, and hoped Hillside lived up to the hype.

Nora plugged in the constellations of tiny white lights strung along the vast windows in the Wild Aster Salon, and the two sets on the rustic Christmas tree they'd fashioned from the trimmings of the big tree in the front parlor and scrub pines and wild hemlocks growing around the property. That little tree, assembled in a wooden planter on the outside walk, boasted decorations in the shapes of ruby-red apples and banana-yellow pears, with strands of red and golden lights woven through its branches. Nora loved the window vignette at the inn's rear entrance almost as much as the main tree, set before the big windows beside the front door.

That tree, wreathed in white and blue lights, garlands of silk flowers, and dried roses, would welcome the first of the inn's guests, due to arrive at any moment.

Music played. The rich aromas of Chef Paul's culinary preparations drifted through the succession of rooms. The scrabble of tires on sanded pavement broke the stagnancy. Long last, the world outside exhaled its icy breath, sending a powdery curtain of snow past the windows.

Three members of a writers' group. A newly married couple from Los Angeles, honeymooning for a week and eager to enjoy the local winter sports scene. A motivational speaker.

Nora drew her heavy winter coat around her, slipped her feet into the wooly boots waiting beside a grapevine basket filled with new pairs of slippers for guests, and hurried out to the car with the New York license plate.

"Welcome to the Hillside," she said.

"Welcome to the North Pole, more like," countered the woman who emerged.

"Guilty as charged. Let me help you with your bags."

Brigid Connelly, the motivational speaker. The Shasta Daisy Suite. Soon after, one of the writers arrived, a pretty bond named Christine, the Prim Rose. The honeymooners, Aaron and Giselle, the Buttercup, pulled into the driveway ahead of an SUV containing the last two members of the writers' group—Karen Jones in the Queen Anne's Lace Room, Roxanne Donner in the Lady's Slipper Suite.

As daylight faded and the world outside the inn's warmth darkened from overcast gray to charcoal, guests gathered in the Wild Aster Salon in ones and twos, introduced themselves, and raised glasses filled with white or claret-red to the finery and fine dining promised by the official opening of the Hillside Inn.

Trays of food appeared in the salon, traveling among guests and the local luminaries who'd signed up for First Night festivities. One of the town's selectmen, Edward Gunderson, snagged a pair of Chef Paul's kicked-up deviled eggs with lemon zest during the first tray pass.

"I love what you've done with the place, Nora," he said. Gunderson bit into the appetizer, rolled his eyes, moaned in approval. "And what your chef is doing with the cuisine!"

"You just wait," she said, and patted the selectman's

shoulder on her way by to check in with Chef Paul on the rest of the night's preparations.

Wind scattered snow and flecks of ice past the salon's windows. En route to the kitchen, Nora dug in her heels and froze. Willing herself to turn took conscious effort. Eventually, she faced left.

The little Christmas tree made from leftover parts on the walkway outside trembled in the mountain wind and scattered liquid light in golden and red drops across the snow. The charcoal skies had deepened almost to black. And somewhere out there, in the new night, Nora swore she caught a quiet flutter of movement, coyly disguised among the powdery snow and wind-stirred branches.

Movement, and Nora was certain, quite certain, that whoever was out there, *whatever*, was staring in at her and her partygoers. The certainty crawled across her flesh, unleashing a shiver. The wind resumed howling.

A host of gourmet treats appeared on the salon's central coffee table: prosciutto crudo, crackers, and slices of a local cheddar served on a slab of black granite; roasted garlic bulbs; grilled asparagus; red pepper seared to perfection; smoked locally-sourced trout with an amazing dill sauce; loaves of crusty bread and herb butter; and cocktail shrimp on ice accompanied by a sharp, homemade cocktail sauce with plenty of fresh horse radish. Bottles of sparkling water stood beside cabernet and pinot. A case of expensive champagne to celebrate the New Year chilled beside the main entrance—waiting for Chef Paul to transfer it into the snow bank an hour before the antique clock on the mantel tolled the arrival of the new year. From there, he would liberate corks from bottles Napoleon-style with a machete blade. All was over-the-top, an experience guaranteed to be remembered.

At eight o'clock, as more tray passes were made and strangers became counterfeit friends by way of their confinement, the local band Nora had hired to play for her guests arrived. She set them up in the corner of the salon bordered by the big windows, with its view of the adorable little Christmas tree made up of leftover parts. Back-lighting the band, the lights of the tree glowed red and gold, and reflected off the surrounding snow.

"Help yourselves to everything," Nora said as acoustic guitars emerged from cases, along with a violin, a tambourine, and even a saw.

"Is there coffee?" the saw-player, a woman who wore rose-colored glasses, asked.

"Yes, over on the bar—regular and decaf."

"Decaf, *blah*," the woman said. "Point me toward the real deal, high octane!"

Nora did. Seconds later, she caught the player of the saw sniffing at the cream pitcher. Then the woman hastily put it down.

"Is something wrong?"

"Yes, the cream's curdled," the saw-player said. "And not just curdled, but crawling with maggots!"

Nora attempted to bury her worry along with her disgust. So the half and half was bad—a lone misstep among so much good. The Hillside Inn positively radiated with joyous laughter, spirited conversation, and music. A countrified version of 'Moon River' floated through the rooms, completed with the Theremin-style quivers produced by the saw.

"How are you doing?" Nora asked the chef.

Paul's usually cheery expression sagged. "Um," he said.

Nora pulled him aside. "What's wrong?"

"Probably better that I show you."

One song ended to applause as he led the way to the kitchen and another began—'Cry Me a River' in smoky, spaced-out fashion. Nora's pulse quickened; suddenly, her heart seemed determined to leap into her throat.

Paul opened the stainless, restaurant-quality fridge and drew out the bowl containing farm fresh eggs—at least a dozen, in their shell.

"I hope I'm wrong this time," said the chef.

Glancing nervously around, he scooted over to the nearest sink. There, he cracked an egg with his usual finesse. But instead of white and sunny yolk, out poured red liquid—what appeared to be blood.

Nora gasped a swear.

"It's all of them," Paul said.

He split another, producing the same result. Nora felt her bile rise. She choked down the foul taste, reached toward the bowl, and cracked an egg. More blood flowed into the sink.

"They were fine this afternoon when I made the deviled eggs," Paul said, though his voice sounded a mile distant.

Nora picked up the bowl and dumped its entire contents into the sink. Shells shattered, the terrible symphony deadened by a crimson massacre.

Wind slithered around the Hillside, carrying icy powder past the front parlor's windows. The ghostly curtains rose and fell, mostly missed by the revelers, but not Nora.

She attempted to forget the growing list of upsets and to remember only the highlights. The guests loved their accommodations, and the inn had seemed to blossom as one year ran out and the next was poised to begin.

"Lovely tree," said a woman's voice at Nora's left.

She turned. Roxanne Donner had delivered the praise.

Nora smiled for the first time since the incident in the kitchen. "Fresh from our very own property," she said. "There are a few acres devoted to Christmas trees, thanks to the previous owner."

"I love it here," Roxanne said. "And the history!"

"You mean the local legend... the witch?"

Roxanne nodded. "Divina Cortland. I read all about her after I booked my stay. I might even write a story about her."

"Be careful," Nora said and chuckled, though the laugh lacked joy. "She might hear you."

"Do you think the ghost of Divina Cortland is present?"

Nora focused on the constellation of tiny blue and white stars woven around the front parlor's Christmas tree. Movement teased her vision. Another clump of pine needles detached and tumbled. Nora blinked and looked lower. The tree's pristine white skirt could barely be gleaned from among the growing layers of dead needles.

"This tree was so alive earlier," she said.

Nora reached toward the nearest branch. An unpleasant symphony jagged in counterpoint to the torchy music being played in the Wild Aster Salon as what had to be hundreds more spilled to the floor.

"Maybe she's here," said Roxanne, whose voice dropped to barely more than a whisper. "The death of live plants is rumored to be a sign."

Nora turned away from the sagging Christmas tree and faced the other woman. "What about cream that goes sour, and fresh eggs with insides transformed to blood?"

Roxanne's eyes widened. "Then I would suggest that we all toss a pinch of salt over our shoulders in the hopes of good luck—and to ward off evil!"

The hour of midnight neared, and Chef Paul readied to pop corks with theatrical flourish. The newlyweds danced, the band performed, and conversations continued as the baleful wind howled around the Hillside Inn.

Nora drew Paul aside. "A slight change of plans."

He listened, clearly not happy.

"Do you have the ingredients?"

"Sure," he said. "But do you really want to do this based upon a couple of crazy mishaps that can probably be explained?"

Nora considered Paul's words. It was crazy. Then she remembered the dead Christmas tree, the blood.

"Witches are allergic to salt," Nora said. "If Divina Cortland is back... "

Paul exhaled through his nostrils. "It's only a story, Nora. But you're the boss."

"And you're the chef. Make them spectacular."

Paul assured her that he would, and retreated to the kitchen.

As midnight ticked closer, the cases of champagne abandoned, he emerged and began to pass among the guests, a serving platter expertly balanced atop his palm. The tray boasted several margarita glasses. He handed one each to the newlyweds, the writers, and the motivational speaker. The next pass took care of the guests, the last musicians, Nora, and Paul himself.

"Everyone," Nora announced. "I'd like to invite you to join me in a new tradition here at the Hillside Inn."

"But it's almost midnight," the motivational speaker said. "What about the bubbly?"

"In due time," Nora said. "First, a toast—to new beginnings. And to old legends staying buried in the past."

"Here, here," someone said.

Glasses were raised. Midnight struck on the antique clock above the mantel. Cheers followed, and the margarita glasses with their salted rims clanged together in celebration. Nora observed the happy scene and instantly suffered a pang at so foolish a concept. Divina Cortland was a tall tale, a cautionary fable told to local children to keep then in line, nothing more.

Right to left—so much joy, in her beautiful inn. It was a new beginning.

Then, as her eyes drifted back toward the right side of the Wild Aster Salon, Nora saw her in the window—the blue-skinned hag with the malevolent expression, standing among the well-dressed party guests, a vision only half there in reflection, a ghost formed by frost that had drifted in past the doors and thresholds.

Somebody screamed.

The frost-woman came apart in a gust of icy wind and snow.

And the door to the outside blew open courtesy of an invisible hand before again slamming shut.

The Witch's Time
Ngo Binh Anh Khoa

Boiling cauldron on dark fire
Bubbles with the witch's ire;
Therein swirls a raging sea,
Black as oceans' depths would be.

From that mixture spreads a smell,
Horrid as her blasphemous spell,
And within the whirlpool dark,
She can hear the magic bark,

Rumbling like a starving beast
Howling for its promised feast;
Hence, the crone at once proceeds
To lay out all that she needs:

Otherworldly herbs she's grown,
Whose names are to none else known,
With dried roots from nether shores
Which she oftentimes explores.

Next are things found in the wild,
Which she's carefully compiled,
"Spiders' legs and lizards' tails,
Gators' teeth and monkeys' nails,

Bones of tigers, fangs of dogs,
Horns of goats and tusks of hogs,
Add some snakes' discarded skin,
Ere the flat worms get thrown in.

Now nine locks of maidens' hair,
Cut off when they once were fair.
Sealed at last with one's own blood,
So the pact stays strong and good."

She then views that lightless pool;
Trembling fingers guide her tool,
Patience waning with the light
Till the heaven's drowned in night.

Under crimson moonlight scant,
She repeats a fervent chant,
"Counter-clockwise stir the brew,
Making Time rewind anew!"

Nether powers further swell
As she shrilly casts her spell;
In a curious tongue long dead,
Strange rhymes are then hoarsely said,

Each sound warring with the gale,
Roaring near her body frail.
Fire crackles, branches cry,
Dead leaves thrash and fall nearby.

Cauldron shrieks and bubbles burst,
Vapors rise ere they're dispersed.
She goes on, determined still,
Pouring in her every will.

Every word's a desperate cry
Of one for whom death is nigh.
Louder, fiercer, madder, then,
Suddenly, all noises end.

In that foul brew of ink-black,
She glares at that which glares back.
With a bowl she takes the broth,
Its brim soaked with teeming froth.

"For a youth regained this day!"
She shouts and drinks it away,
Downing that repulsive taste,
Caution banished in her haste.

Once she's done, she'd stand and wait
To see if she's altered fate.
Minutes pass with no effect,
Not a change can she detect.

Shards of ice now stab her heart
As despair tears her apart.
But it'd soon abruptly come,
Rendering her whole being numb.

Magic bursts forth from within,
Smoldering her core therein.
She can feel it in her veins,
Bringing with it harrowing pains.

As though Hellfire's blazing there,
Sweltering, too much to bear.
She keels over, quivering,
Trapped in grueling suffering.

Hotter grows her temperature,
Deathly feverish without cure,
But when she thinks she will die,
Old Death never once stops by.

Damned to Agony's rending claw
For perverting Nature's Law,
No reprieve the witch would know;
Conscious thoughts fast come and go.

She soon neither speaks nor moves,
Even breathing strenuous proves.
Thus, she lies still, nothing more
Than a gasping fish ashore.

Endless is the torture's length,
Robbing her of fading strength
Through the cold and lonesome night,
Till the heaven's once more bright.

Long extinguished is her fire,
And long doused her vain desire.
Silent has the cauldron grown,
Blackened, lifeless and alone.

Bubbles swell, less than before,
Less and less, and then, no more.

Both Sides Now
C. I. I. Jones

Greg parked his car up the street from the apartment and let it idle. You could never find a spot in front of the building. Never. He always parked a block away and walked. He pressed his phone to his ear.

"The flight's about to take off," Lily said. "I need to go soon."

Greg let out an oversized moan of despair. "Please! Please don't go!" he begged his wife.

"Give it a rest. I'll be home before you know it." They both laughed.

"I know. I'll be fine."

And he did know it, but in the five years they'd been together, they'd spent less than twenty days apart. And now, with Lily's mom sick in New Jersey, he was looking at a ten-day stretch. Ten lonely days. And for what? Lily's bitch of a mother hadn't even shown at the wedding. Five years, and he'd never even met her. And what did Lily do? Make excuses. *Oh, we're very close but weddings just aren't her thing.* Really?

"You're pitiful," Lily said. "You should take advantage of the time, Greg. You never get time alone.

"I guess that's true," he muttered.

"And if you get too bored you can just ask the scarecrow lady to come over."

They both had a good laugh over this. "Not a chance," said Greg. "She scares the hell outta me."

"Be nice. She's just a lonely old lady. You're gonna know how she feels this week, old man."

"True enough."

"Cheer u—" but Lily cut herself off. Greg could hear a distant voice that he took for the airport P.A. system. "I gotta go, hun, I love you." she said quickly.

"I love you t—" but the call disconnected, and Greg's week alone was underway. He swallowed the lump in his throat and told himself he really was pitiful. He turned the car off. The only sound on the street was his clicking engine as it cooled.

Good, he thought. It must be getting too cold for the scarecrow lady to play outside. His thought was confirmed as he opened the door and cool fall air seeped into the peaceful cocoon of the heated car.

He stretched his legs onto the street and pulled himself out of the car. It was getting dark too early, he thought. Their street wasn't the most dangerous in the city, far from it, but he hated walking it alone at night. His face flushed at the thought. Why the hell, at 37, was he still doing this? Shouldn't he and Lily have a house in some boringly safe neighborhood? He started the walk back to his apartment. No kids, he told himself. Too much space, he added. Somewhere in the back of his mind he could hear Lily saying that they just couldn't afford it. All these things were only half-truths. They could afford it, it'd be tight, but they could. Too much space meant filling space, which could be fun to do. No kid was something that he and his wife didn't think about. Didn't want to think about it. Lily wasn't able to. Simple as that. Lily took it hard. The love was still there, but it had taken its toll. Especially with the sex. It's not all about procreation, thank God, but it's part of the thing. It was an ominous cloud in their marriage, ready to rain on them at any second. A dark figure lurking from their perch ready to pounce, just like—

Greg reached his apartment. The building was old, built in the 1920s, and had the classic layout of city apartments. Each unit had six apartments on three floors. The stairs inside led up to a first-floor landing. To the right or left were apartments one and two. Turn and go up two more flights of stairs, you have three and four, and after the last flight of stairs, five and six. Greg and Lily lived in apartment four. The second floor on the right. The perfect spot for getting to know your neighbors, sandwiched between floors three and one.

Greg should have been walking inside to climb the three flights of stairs to home-sweet-home in apartment four, but he was frozen. He felt her eyes. He could always feel her eyes scouring the street from apartment five. She perched up there all day. They called her scarecrow lady because of the burlap texture of her face. She wore heavy makeup, with blood-red lipstick. Even if she was frowning, her lipstick gave the look of a ghoulish half smile.

On nights, not cold ones like this, but the kind that come in spring or early fall, she would play. Cello. An aging concert cellist, out on her balcony, the world and her neighbors her audience, willing or not. Greg wasn't willing.

"She freaks me out," he told his wife a month after the scarecrow woman moved in. It was only a week since they learned Lily was barren. A weird neighbor was a great relief to talk about. In the first three hours she occupied the space, she was out on the balcony, playing what would be her usual concert. One long, sustained note. Played to perfection, for ten minutes. Greg knew nothing about music, but he knew this wasn't normal. People played songs, not long-lasting hums of string.

"Oh, take it easy," Lily told him. "She's probably just lonely. That cello is probably her last living friend."

"She could at least play a whole song. Instead of notes. For ten minutes straight," then he added to himself, "The old scarecrow."

Lily eeked with laughter, then guiltily whispered, "It's so true. She does kind of look like one." And with that, the name stuck.

Outside his apartment, Greg could feel her, peering down in the darkness; searching him out like she always did when he walked by. Like a guard in a watchtower always searching for one specific con in the yard. In the days when weather permitted, when those long, sustained notes from the cello carried on the wind, up the street to wherever Greg parked, he prepared himself for the evening routine. The long sustained cello notes as he made his way to the door, and then sudden silence. Then, her eyes peering down. Peeking out from that leathery skin, her face like a pie crust and the eyes like two shriveled cherries.

He looked up then, sure that he was about to meet those eyes, but it was too dark, and he couldn't see the top half of the building. He half expected her eyes to catch a glint of moonlight and flash down on him.

In the years since the scarecrow lady moved in, the theories Greg and Lily shared about her ranged from the plausible to the downright bizarre. The one Greg developed about her being some sort of night creature, hungry for flesh raced through his mind. Cat eyes from above staring down at him. Wondering how the fleshy part of his neck might feel in her mouth.

The image put Greg's feet in motion. He walked inside the apartment building. God, I wish Lily were here, he thought. Her theories on the Scarecrow Lady were always endearing, or heart breaking, never veering to the fantastic. He tried to think of one as he walked up the first flight of stairs. *She was a Hungarian refugee, her family lost in some awful war. She plays the one note on the cello over and over again because it reminds her of her daughter, that was only beginning to learn the scales.* Of course, Hungarian wasn't right. Greg knew that. Or if she was, she did a fine job masking her accent. He made his way up the first flight of stairs. How did he know she wasn't Hungarian? He knew because of the day they met on the stairs.

He was possibly the only person in the building who spoke to her, and it happened right here on these stairs. It was a memory he tried to forget. He never told his wife. It seemed useless to tell her. It'd give her one more reason to think he's a joke. Low-paying job. Scared of little old ladies. It'd probably slow down the progress of finally moving out of the apartment until the ripe age of 53. But it happened right here.

He came home sick with a light fever. He probably could have worked through it, but the office was slow that day, so why not? The fever grew and by the time he was parking up the street from the apartment, he was shivering. Good call to come home. He walked the block toward his end of the building. It was a nice day, and he was surprised to not hear the cello. It was early fall and the kids on the block were at school, but surely the scarecrow lady was at home.

He walked through the front door of the building and was checking the mailbox when he thought he heard soft footsteps on one of the flights of stairs above him. He looked up, through the gap between the zig-zags of railing going up to the third floor, half-expecting to see a child looking back at him. There was nobody there, so he resumed flipping through the mail, tossing any garbage to the trashcan provided specifically for junk mail before returning to their apartment. Greg started up the first flight of stairs with his fever boiling to furnace level, then he heard it again.

Wiping sweat from his brow, he leaned over to look up the gap again, and this time he saw a movement; the flick of a woman's long hair, or the sudden flash of color from a bright summer dress of a lady rounding the corner; it was gone too quick to tell.

Some fever, he thought, and started up the next flight. This time the patter of feet was gone. It was replaced by four big thuds on the stairs, THUMP—THUMP—THUMP—THUMP—as if the person coming down the stairs was jumping down, one at a time. Greg thought they must be on the landing between the second and third floor, and he began to feel uneasy.

He was thinking he preferred not to meet whoever those heavy footsteps belonged to. Despite his warnings to himself, he peeked up the gap again. This time his eyes locked with the sunken cherry eyes of the scarecrow lady. She giggled, and it wasn't the laugh of an old crone like he'd always imagined. It was a girl's laugh, a girl at play.

He moved quicker then, annoyed by the idea of a stairwell encounter while on the verge of passing out from his fever. The old lady wasn't a terror; just a little off in the old noggin. Nothing to be afraid of, but he certainly didn't want to have a conversation with the strangest of his neighbors. He took the next flight up two at a time.

THUMP—THUMP—the entire staircase shook as the scarecrow lady came down, matching his pace. That girlish laugh followed, and then a mutter, seemed to come from the back of her throat. She was speaking, though Greg couldn't make the words out. He didn't give a shit what she was saying, could be the Lord's Prayer, for all he knew. His fever was growing, and so was his desire to avoid this nut job. He put his head down and shambled up the last flight. But there she stood, between him and his door.

She muttered again. It came from the back of her throat like before, but this time he was close enough. He could not just hear the words, but smell them, he breath wafting over his nose with the smell of aged milk and onions.

"I know you," she said, then smiled. "Always known you, boy."

The voice was high pitched and northeastern. Not quite Boston, not quite New York, but somewhere in between. "I know you," she said again.

Greg looked down at her feet to avoid the eyes, the face, the one he'd made terrible jokes about with his wife. "Uh, yeah. Of course you do. We're neighbors." He thought about reaching his hand out to shake hers, but thought better of it and left his clammy hand pinned to his side.

"No," she responded. "I know you from way further back than that. I know you deep down. I've had you."

Now Greg looked into the eyes, buried in her burlap face, wishing he could throw her out of the way and flee through his door. Still, he couldn't help himself, couldn't hold back the words.

"You had me?"

She'd leaned in closer, and the putrid smell flooded his nostrils and he could feel hot bile climbing up his throat.

"Oh yes. I've had you. I will have you again," she wheezed in that accent.

American, not Hungarian, he thought. Lily would like to know that. His keys came out of his pocket and plinked off the aged wood floor of the landing. She grabbed his shoulders before he could bend to grab them.

"Your wife, she won't care. I'll have you, yes! I will pull this right off your lap with my teeth."

She grabbed his crotch and, inches away from his face let her tongue loll out of her mouth and around her cracked lips. The stench grew worse as he realized it was her rotting teeth. The small glimpse he allowed himself revealed brown teeth splitting out of a black gum line. His balls scrunched up like dates. The bile in his mouth was just inside his own clenched lips.

He bent to grab his keys, shoving the scarecrow lady forward a pace to make room. When he stood back up, she was eye-to-eye with him, so close they were splitting molecules of oxygen.

"Don't you be afraid, boy. It's happened all through time. I've had you, ate you all up, time and time again, forever and ever."

She kissed him then, long and hard, her bony hands grasping either side of his face. The air that should have been burning through his throat and out of his nose was getting sucked out of him. The bile slipped through his lips and down her throat, and when she pushed him away, it was through his own apartment door. She shut the door for him, and he stared dumbly at the paneling, listening to the soft thud of footsteps as she ascended to her third-floor apartment.

All of it happened in a matter of seconds, right here where Greg was standing two years later. On the second-floor landing in front of his apartment. He never told Lily. Would she believe him? Standing here now he barely believed it himself. A fever? An illusion? Maybe. But the smell was too real to forget. Rotting milk and onions. As he stood before his door, searching for his keys, he couldn't help but listen for footsteps on the third-floor landing.

The keys jingled in his hands, and he fumbled through them to find the right one. He worked himself into a frenzied sweat, and his hand-eye coordination seemed to shrink as his fear grew. Finally, he found the key, plunged into the lock and twisted. The lock turned over and he shouldered the door as he turned the knob, expecting to fly into his apartment. But the door traveled all of an inch and stopped cold. The chain lock was pulled to, and a sliver of light leaked into his living room, just enough to see the gray fabric on the armrest of their couch.

"Jesus Christ, Lily!" he hissed to himself.

And his panic of being accosted by their freak of a neighbor gave way to frustration. How many times had he told her the same thing? Don't leave the chain on the front door. If you leave out the back, make sure to unchain the front door so that he can get inside when he gets home. A simple request that was granted only 50 percent of the time.

"Shit," he muttered.

The anger subsided, and the truth of a few lonely days came back. At least, most days when this happened, she was on the other side of the door, apologizing, and rushing through their home to let him in. Always with a kiss waiting for him. Not tonight though, he thought. He'd have to go around back.

When he moved back toward the stairs, he knew he heard a squeak from above, the weight of that woman moving upstairs. His pace down the stairs quickened, and as he reached the bottom his feet almost tangled, sending him sprawling, but he caught his balance and burst back out of the door and onto the sidewalk in front of their building. No moon showing that night, which was good, he thought. He didn't care to look up and find that he was right about his feeling. That she was perched there, watching him, waiting for the right time to *have* him. Spewing her hot breath into the frigid night.

He managed to fight the urge to run around to the back of the building. A man must keep his dignity after all. So he walked, briskly, and made the corner, all the while feeling her eyes burning into the back of his head, whether she was there or not didn't matter. He felt it. He walked to the base of his own unit's fire escape and looked up. No light came from the back of the building. Nobody home in any of the apartments. Fine, he thought, as he grabbed the rusted handrail. As he took the first step he heard it. A single note; the bow pulled across taut strings, causing the cello somewhere up there in the dark to moan. A long and sustained moan. Greg stopped three steps up, and had a difficult time swallowing, the last gulp of air stuck in his throat. He coughed, and as the cough echoed through the empty lot behind the building, the cello moan was gone.

He took the next three steps together, already holding his keys, searching for the back door key by the memory of its shape. The fire escape staircase twisted, spiraling up to the second floor. His floor. The safety of his and Lily's home. Could he hear the cello moaning again though? Was it getting closer? Of course, it is you moron, he told himself, you are going closer to it with each step!

But, on the second floor, keys in hand, fumbling with the lock, there was no soundtrack to his struggle. Just city noises off in the distance and his breathing, constantly hitching in his throat like he was about to sneeze. No cello.

The key twisted in the lock, and again he put his shoulder to the door and pushed. He certainly couldn't breathe now, as again, a chain pulled taut on the back door and his entrance, his attempt to tag home was cut short. "What the hell?" he whined. And it was a whine, but more than that, a genuine question. Lily is gone, he thought. If both chains are pulled, how in the hell did she leave? Shimmy down the fucking balcony?

His fear now at blinding levels, he pictured himself leaning back on the rusty handrail of the fire escape and taking his foot to the door. One good kick would do the trick. Then he pictured explaining this to his wife. The last bit of his pride faded like the red glint in the sky at sunset. His fear was always a little stronger than his pride. He leaned back, poised to kick the door, when he heard her.

"Oh, there you are," the whisper came. "I've been waiting for so, so long." The voice moaned from just inside the door, sounding just as ominous and loathsome as the long cello notes. "I'm so sorry I locked you out, boy." He could smell her rotting gums from where he stood outside, drifting through the crack in the door, cut off suddenly as the door shut.

You should run, he told himself. Hell, you should jump off the side of this fire escape if that's what it takes to get away from this psycho. But he was rooted. Even the sound of the chain lock sliding out of its catch in the door didn't cause him to move. The doorknob twisting and the door opened. There stood the scarecrow lady, framed in pure black, in his apartment. His feet didn't twitch, his whole body waited for her to walk from the darkness.

She spoke. "Aren't you coming in?

"I—I—" but he was unable to make coherent thoughts become coherent words.

"Jesus, Greg! I'm trying to do something here! Are you coming in or not?"

The tone of the voice had changed, there was no sulphury breath spewing from his dark doorway. And the silhouette his adjusting eyes was starting to make out lifted its arm out closer to him, enough to make the details of the hand. Not claws, or even the old cracked skin and chipped fingernails of the scarecrow lady.

Lily stepped forward enough for him to recognize her, and to recognize that she barely had any clothing on. What little clothing she did have on had its own purpose, and it wasn't to cover any of her up.

"God, Greg! It's freezing. And I don't know if you can see me very well, but I don't have much on to keep me warm. Get in here!" she squeaked with a laugh.

"I—uh, yeah I can see you," Greg murmured.

He took her outstretched hand. They both went inside. She reached behind him and closed the door to the fire escape.

"Yeah? You like what you see?"

"I heard someone else," Greg said, sounding far away, still trying to grasp what was going on. "Wait a sec. Why are you here? You're supposed to be with your—"

"All a ruse," Lily said and touched him on the nose. "I wanted to try something new. Things have maybe been a bit stale, right?"

"So you didn't go to Jersey?"

Lily laughed. "Does it look like I went to Jersey?"

Greg looked her up and down. No, it certainly didn't look like she'd gone to Jersey. And he was starting to realize that was very good for him.

"But your mom? Is she okay?"

"I'm sure she is. What's it matter anyway? You said you'd never want to meet her when she didn't show for the wedding."

"Sure, but she's your mother after all."

"You want to talk about my mother for foreplay," she said, grabbing his hand and guiding it to her thigh, up and down the black silk number she was wearing.

No, he didn't want to talk about her mother.

"Come on," she whispered.

She tugged at his hand and led him back to their bedroom. A soft warm glow from candles placed around the room illuminated them. Their bed, which usually sat in the corner, was pulled to the center of the room. How the hell had she done that alone?

"Really went all out, huh?" Greg said with a smirk.

"Something like that," Lily agreed. "Why don't you get comfortable on the bed. I've got some finishing touches to add, and then I'll be right back."

Without answer, Lily left the room and shut the door behind her.

Get comfortable, Greg thought. Okay, get comfortable. More than comfortable though, he was excited. His wife really had pulled one over on him. That's fun. Also, the sexual curveball was a page out of Lily's playbook that was actively in use early on in their relationship, but one that Greg had assumed she long ago discarded. Especially in the couple years since they discovered she couldn't have kids.

He took his pants and shirt off, only leaving his boxers on, and lay on the bed. He stared at the ceiling for a while, wondering what had stirred up his wife. Don't question these things, came the answer inside of his head. Roll with it. Enjoy it!

Sure, sure, he thought. Enjoy it. What a rush, was his next thought. In a matter of five minutes, he'd gone from lonely and sad, to deathly afraid (which at this moment, seemed so ludicrous as to make him giggle), to grateful. Grateful for his wife that loved him so well.

He looked at the candles. Lily always kept some handy, something he also loved about his wife. The apartment always smelled so good. Cotton scent in the bathroom. Coffee with hazelnut in the kitchen. But these, he couldn't quite catch the scent, or if there was any scent to catch at all. Five candles in a room, and no scent seemed odd. Not like Lily to buy candles that are purely decorative. Stop, stop, he told himself. Then aloud, said, "It's just part of the set up. Something nice."

The door creaked open slowly, and he could hear the floorboards shifting under her weight.

"I was wondering where you were," he said, still not looking toward her, just straight up at the ceiling.

"Was beginning to wonder if I'd dreamt the whole thing and you really did go to Jersey."

He got a scent then, though he knew it wasn't the candles. The five black candles spilling wax onto five distinct points of the floor around the room. The smell was rotten milk and onions, and he smelt it as he heard her say,

"No, my boy. You are not dreaming," in that accent. Distinctly American. No New York, no Boston. But perhaps, New Jersey.

He scrambled up on his arms, poised to jump off the bed. But his arms were yanked out from under him. Lily stood over top of him, at the head of the bed. He hadn't noticed quite a few things in the room since he arrived. The colors of the candles, for one, which were black. The faint five-pointed star etched into the floorboards, just barely visible in the light of the candles. He didn't notice the straps affixed to the bedposts, the straps that his wife had already yanked around his wrists. She stared down at him, solemn, but with no remorse.

The scarecrow lady walked over. "My love, your husband is such a handsome boy," she crooned, just like a note out of her wretched cello. "One of the family. Your father would be so proud."

"Lily," Greg twisted in the bed. "Lily, what the fuck are you doing?"

"It's what we need," Lily said somberly. "It will help us, my love. It's the only way that you can be one with me. That we can be one together. Share each other."

"What do you mean?" Greg moaned.

"I told you I would have you boy," the scarecrow lady said, mounting the bed, her knees on each side of Greg's waist. From somewhere in her dark robe, she produced a knife, and ran it across her palm, smooth, with no sign discomfort in her face. "I told you, and I told her. And now you see, that mother keeps her word. Isn't that right, sweet Lily."

"It is, mother," Lily said from a point in the room where Greg couldn't see her.

"Yes, it is true," Greg's mother in-law repeated. The blood began to fill her palm and dripped down off of her wrist onto Greg's chest. She began speaking in some ancient language that Greg could not place. Lily repeated the same incantations of a dead language long ago abandoned for its evil uses. Yes, he couldn't place the language, but he could certainly hear that New Jersey accent.

The Way of Wishes
Claire Davon

The face emerging from the hut was ugly in the way of all old people. Her skin was far more wrinkled than anyone I had ever seen and a few moles dotted her cheeks. I tried not to stare at one of them that had hair coming out of its center. Her hook nose was almost bulbous at the tip. Straggly grey hair fell across her neck and chest

"Are you the witch who grants wishes?"

The witch cackled, the sound turning into a dry, rasping cough as she cleared the door. Her body was skinny and sunken, the parts of her arms I could see little more than bone and liver spotted skin. Her feet were covered in thick shoes that were worn in the soles and toes. Her clothing, ragged and torn, was nonetheless clean, if mended repeatedly.

She stood in front of me, a staff in one hand. She looked me up and down and I thought I saw disapproval in her face. I kept my own neutral. Even through the forest pine I could smell her scent, a hint of smoke mixed with herbs. Witches' brew, no doubt.

"Depends on the wish," she said.

It was said that if the witch caught you in the woods she would skin and eat you. She was said to have powers that were deadly, or helpful, depending on her whim. The foolish or desperate sought her out.

I was the latter, and also the former.

Her log hut had gaps between the hewn wood. The only access into or out of the building was via the door that she had emerged from. A tabby cat now appeared from that same door and stared at me from the opening. I heard barking from the inside.

"You are the witch Sofya, are you not?"

She looked me up and down and sniffed. My insides quivered, though I showed no expression. The faint of heart did not succeed with witches.

"If you are trying to win favors from me you are going

about it in a peculiar way. Rudeness wins no allies," she said, resting her weight on the staff. It was thicker on one end than the other and was made of grey wood.

"I beg your pardon," I said. "I do seek a favor. I understand you grant them. Is that not the case?"

She gazed up at me before chuckling and thumping her staff on the ground in a surprisingly strong whack. Dirt eddied from underneath and somewhere above birds screeched.

"That's better," she said though her lips were pursed. "As for a favor... we shall see. Make yourself useful. I need water. Fetch it."

She gestured to two water buckets standing near the side of the hut. They were bone dry, their handles worn and dirty, like so much of the witch. Leaves cascaded around their bottoms and it looked as though they had not been used in a while.

"Of course, Madame Sofya. At once," I said, after the silence had gone on a beat or two too long. I was not going about this well. If I angered her, then I had no hope of being granted my favor.

I took the buckets and set out. The brook was further away than I anticipated, and the pails weighed more than I thought. I dipped first one and then the other into the water, filling the pails enough to bring them back full but without slopping the water over. Somehow I knew it would not do any good to bring them back half empty.

My chore done, I struggled back to the hut, the weight of the buckets making the going slow. Leaves crunched underfoot and there was always the possibility of moss, or snails, to make the way slick. If I fell, I would have to start again and I wanted nothing to delay me.

When I got back the witch was peering in my direction. "Come come," she said when she laid eyes on me. "I have meat in the pot. Bring those in." She scurried inside, not waiting for my reply.

I eyed the building, wondering if it was wise to go in there. I thought of the boy in the Baba Yaga legend, who had been lured into her hut by the promise of an apple. Things had not turned out well for him. Still, I had come this far and if I meant to get my wish I had to show no fear.

I nodded, swallowing my concern.

I was mad to attempt this. Few came back with successful tales. It was said the witch would slay you if she found you to be false or impure of heart. How she knew I did not know but witches had ways that were not known to common folk. My quest was not dishonest, but I wasn't pure minded. Only the rich had that luxury.

It took several moments for my thudding heart to stop long enough for me to compose my face before I entered. I hauled one heavy bucket in before setting it down and bringing the other.

She showed no sign of acknowledging my entrance. She was stirring something on the cooktop. The aroma of a stew filled my nostrils, reminding me that it had been a long time since I'd eaten.

It might not be too late to flee. I had not asked her for my favor and she might let me go. It was impossible to know the outcome if I attempted it. Then I had nothing to look forward to but a desperate existence eking out what living I could on my too-small patch of ground. My life would for sure be a misery. This was my only chance. I could not falter now.

I cleared my throat and stepped all the way into the room, holding my breath to see what would happen.

Winter had not yet taken hold of the landscape but it was far enough in that I wondered how the witch Sofya got the vegetables and tomatoes I saw in the pot. She bustled about, saying nothing else for several minutes. I shifted from side to side, wanting to break the silence but fearing the consequences if I did so.

The cat launched itself off its perch and onto the floor. Startled, I backed away, then heard a yelp. A small dog growled from where it had been laying. The cat gave the dog a swat and then pranced off, its tail held high.

Several more minutes passed while I exhausted all observation of the cabin. Besides the stove, there was a storage cabinet, a tiny bed with a threadbare cover and a walled off place. Anything could be there, but I could make nothing out.

Still she said nothing. She put the spoon to her cracked lips and tasted the broth. She smacked them and then, appearing satisfied, moved the giant pot to a cooler burner. She showed no strain when she lifted it.

"Well, *maladoi chilavek*, I admit you have been very patient." She pointed toward me. "I do not get visitors without an objective. State your reason for visiting Sofya."

She turned her gaze on me and her eyes were so cold I flinched. She seemed to grow three sizes. Her presence took over the space and her eyes glittered with an inner light. I drew back, thinking of the door and freedom.

But she had agreed to hear my plea and that was all I could ask for. I could not balk at the first sight of adversity.

"Uh," I stammered. "Um," I said again. I'd had a week to perfect my plea but now that I was here all I'd practiced fled.

"Out with it, or you will join the rabbit in this pot. There is not much fat to you but you can add flavor to the stew."

Her cat and dog would make better meat. I kept my face still, afraid to give away my thoughts.

"You are right. I'm here to beg a favor from you. I, er, um, I... there is this girl... "

"There always is," she interrupted with a harsh sound. "Who is this woman?"

It seemed so easy when I was walking here. "Dominikais, the daughter of the local merchant. She is the prettiest around, and the woman I want to marry. Her father will decide soon, and there are many offers for her hand. I have no hope, unless a miracle happens. I wish for you to make her father choose me."

Her burning gaze raked over me for long moments. I tried not to fidget.

"What is your name, *maladoi chilavek*?"

I breathed out a sigh of relief. It had to be a good sign she was asking. Predators didn't need to know the name of their prey.

"Pyotr, Madame Sofya. I am named for my father. Pyotr Khlopov."

Her chuckle held a hint of malice, or perhaps amusement.

"As I thought. You are a peasant. What does this young woman, this *devushka*, have to send you to me to beg a favor of her?" She ladled out a bit of the stew into bowls and set them on the floor next to the cat and dog. She offered none to me.

"She is the loveliest girl in our village," I said.

That earned me another dry laugh and she once again fixed her gaze on me. I could not see her expression. I was pretty sure I did not want to.

"Well, Pyotr, you have caught me at an indulgent moment. I would have you perform three tasks and if you complete them I will give you a gift to take back to your village to claim this Dominika."

I stared at her in disbelief. The challenges would be formidable, and I could fail. But I had a chance.

"I... thank you, Madame. It is more than I could ask for."

"Yes," she agreed, her ancient face creasing into a smile. "It is. Come. Listen to your first mission."

The first task seemed simple enough—chop down enough wood to fill the space next to her hut but no matter how much I chopped the pieces never accumulated. I would load up the area and then the pile would vanish. My arms and legs ached with the effort but I kept on it. Over time the heap started to grow. After several days she swooped down and declared the chore complete.

The second task, to supply her larder with meat, was harder. I hunted for days with little to show for it. When I had begun to despair I lucked upon a moose. I was able to slay the beast and wrestle it to the witch's hut. Then she told me I had to cut it up. It was bloody work but I set to the task. When I finished she grunted and nodded that it was sufficient.

"Are you ready for your third and final test?"

I began to be hopeful. These tasks were difficult but not impossible. I could do it. Whoever said she burdened her seekers with unmanageable errands was wrong. Much of what I had been told about her was incorrect.

"I am at your service."

She studied me for a long time. There was something strange and secretive about her countenance. I told myself she was nothing but an old crone. I would do this chore and be gone. Once I was away I would tell the world that the witch Sofya was not so fearful as all that. If she were what the legends claimed then she would know I was not pure of heart and I would be dead. Since I was not, she had to be less than she appeared.

None of my thoughts showed on my face as I waited to hear what my final job would be. I no longer feared her reading my mind. Marrying Dominika was a practical move. Love was a luxury that I could not afford. It might come in time, but if it didn't that was unimportant. Without her father's resources I had nothing. With her I would have shelter and the promise of a future. Her father was not a rich man, but he was richer than I.

"Your third and final task is to procure me a flame from the heart of Elbrus. The mountain is a week's travel there and a week back so you had better go. Time grows short."

I did a quick calculation out the phases of the moon and groaned at the time involved.

"Yes, Madame Sofya. Then I will return home to the woman I would marry."

She smiled. "How do you know the maiden will be there when you return?"

I pointed to the sky. "Her father will make his choice at the full moon. I have to be back by then to claim my place by her side."

Sofya's lips spread over her crooked teeth in a parody of a smile.

"Then you must be off. Time grows short."

There was nothing left to say. I took the torch she handed me, tucked it into my pack and set off.

Even running it took several days. Once I got there I climbed to the top. Once at the summit I despaired getting a flame out of it. The volcano was dormant and its fire banked. I searched up and down the rocks, to no avail.

After a day's searching I found a cave with a glow at the back. I proceeded down, following the radiance for several hundred yards. Deep inside I reached a small flow of molten rock that was the source of the light and lit the flame. I struggled to contain my glee. This task, like the others before it, hadn't been impossible. Soon I would have a comfortable life and respect in our small village.

I slept little on my journey back, always fearful that the

torch would go out and I would have to return for a new flame. Every day was a day closer to the day of selection.

When I arrived at the hut the dog gave me a baleful look. It had shown little interest in me in the past but now barked in fierce yaps.

The witch stuck her head through the open door as she had on that first day, her head and body covered by her cloak. I thought I detected a flicker of surprise.

"Pyotr, you have returned," she said and seemed to flow over the ground to where I stood. She took the flame and then looked at me. The dog loped over to her and she handed the fire to him. Holding it in his mouth, the dog raced into the hut. His gaze was on me the entire way, something knowing in that stare.

Her eyes were hooded, her expression hidden. Gooseflesh erupted over my body and I fought to keep from rubbing my arms. I didn't want to meet her gaze, but the witch cleared her throat and I had to look at her.

There was something moving behind her face, but whether the emotion was amusement or anger that I had achieved my goals I could not tell. She threw her hood back and her grey hair was a wild tangle under the cloth.

"I see you are waiting for your reward. Here it is. The charm will make Dominika's father choose you as her husband. But beware. This will have nothing less than the joining of your life to hers. Are you sure of your path?"

I held my hand out, trying to control a snort of disgust. "You are mad because I succeeded where you were sure I would fail." I could be scornful now that I had done my errands. "Give me what I came for, or I will tell the world that Madame Sofya does not fulfill her promises."

Her gaze narrowed and her lips thinned. "I ask you again, Pyotr, are you sure you want this charm?"

"Give it to me and be done," I said, holding out my hand. Despite myself, I quivered under her penetrating stare.

"I ask you a third time. Are you sure?"

"I am sure, witch."

"So be it." She drew a small cloth doll from her cloak, with a piece of my hair stitched onto the head. Something flowed over her face, full of screams and dead things. She murmured words over it. I shifted, impatient to be away.

Then she handed it to be and I snatched it from her. I tucked the charm away in a pouch inside my shirt.

"You will return to the village within a week and give this to her. It will be the day of the full moon, as you have indicated was necessary. Understand that if you fail you will die. That is the price of this talisman."

"I understand, Madame Sofya. Thank you."

She cackled, the sound raising the hairs on the back of my neck. "Come inside," she said, gripping my wrist and hauling me over to the table in the corner.

"Is there another task you wish me to perform?" I did not want to delay yet something held me firm. The fact that she'd enchanted the trinket told me that she was not powerless.

She chuckled again, her face twisted. My heart began a trip hammer beat, pounding so loud I imagined she could hear. All the legends battered my brain, my fear lending them strength.

"Your tasks are at an end, Pyotr. I thought you would like to know your fortune before you go."

There was knowledge in her eyes that made me pause. I saw her face harden as I hesitated. She could even now grab the charm away from me, or make it lose its potency. I nodded without enthusiasm.

"Yes, I would like to know my future."

She held her hand out and I placed mine crosswise over her papery palm. She closed bony fingers around my hand. Looking down I could see blue veins beating under the skin. Up close she smelled like smoke and herbs.

Images flowed into my mind. I flinched, trying to snatch my hand away. She gripped me with surprising force.

"I see a big place a weeks' walk from here," she said.

"It must be the town down the road from my village," I said."I have never been there but I understand it is grand. Too grand for one such as me."

"I see," she said her fingers a vise on my palm. I began to sweat, her words sending spears of cold terror up my spine. I looked around and saw the dog standing a few feet away from us, his hackles raised and showing teeth. I dared not move.

"I see you there," she said, her voice rough. "I see you

making a great name for yourself in the town. You will open a shop and it will be successful."

I saw a house with many bedrooms, where children played in the yard. By the curve of the noses there was no doubt they were my offspring. My wife was at my side as I looked out over my land. One look at her beautiful face and I was in love. She was not Dominika.

She stopped talking. I gasped at the beauty of the visions. "Thank you, Madame Sofya, for showing me my fortune. It... it is more than I could hope for. I will set off at once for the town."

Her cool fingers stopped me, their grip hard on my skin. "Have you so soon forgotten the charm?"

I stared at her. "What?"

She gestured as though she could see the vision. "This is what you sacrificed when you asked for a trinket to obtain Dominika."

"No. It cannot be. It is my future. I..." I broke off when her cackle rose until I wanted to clap my hands over my ears.

"It *was* your future, Pyotr, but no longer. Did nobody warn you of the dangers of seeking Madame Sofya?"

Dread spread through my body. I stared at her in disbelief.

"I did as you asked," I said, shivers running through my body although the hut was hot. "Why is this not my outcome?"

Now she met my gaze and her eyes were cold. "Only those with pure intentions get their wish from me," she said, her voice ringing through the small room. "I knew yours were far from innocent. I could have slain you but instead I laid a trap for you and you fell into it. I asked you three times and you agreed as many. You have no choice but to wed Dominika else you will die. You wanted this and now it is yours."

The charm was a heavy weight in my coat where just moments before it had been welcome. I thought about the life I had seen. It would have been mine but for this damned witch.

"I'll throw it away or burn it. You cannot make me do this."

"You would die when you did so, Pyotr Khlopov. I gave you your wish. Now you must fulfill the charm's intent or die." She pointed a finger at me. "Did you not wonder why my tasks took so little effort?"

The cat meowed and stretched. It opened its mouth and hissed in a slow gesture.

"The tasks were difficult," I protested. "I performed the chores you set out. I do not deserve this."

She grew, blocking all sides of the hut until all I could see was her. I shrank back, my mouth dry, my pulse racing.

"You dare?" Her voice came from above me. "You come here with a heart full of greed and say I am being unfair? Come to Madame Sofya with a pure heart and I may grant your wish. Come to me with selfish motives, and you get what you deserve."

"Do not do this. Please. I beg you." I grasped for something, anything. "I will bring you whatever you desire. Just let me go."

She flowed down back to her normal size. If I ran I had no choice of releasing the spell. Now that I had seen my bright future I did not want to lose it.

"I do not have need of things such as you could bring, young man. Your fate is sealed. Be gone with you Pyotr Khlopov. You are a warning to those who seek out the witch for selfish reasons. Never pursue me again. You will die if you do so."

I was flung out of the cabin and tumbled to the leafy forest. Dazed, I looked over to see the structure rising in the air. The hut did a sharp turn and flew away, the wind whistling behind it as it left. As I watched it got smaller and then was gone.

After a moment the normal echoes of the deep woods resumed. Birds chirped around me. I heard the rustling of bugs under my feet and in the distance the movement of small animals.

I began a slow jog home. I was trapped like a rabbit in a snare. I half expected to see the witch swoop down in her hut, but I realized it mattered not. Whether I defied her and died or lived a life of misery mattered not to her.

The charm was a heavy weight inside my coat, although it was a mere fraction of a pound. I had tried to change my fate and made it worse. Madame Sofya gave me what I asked for and doomed me in the process.

The life I saw in the spell swam in my vision. I thought again of the big house, the three children and the wife who was not Dominika. I ached for my true spouse, and my babies.

I reached the crossroads. The path to the town was one direction, the village another. I paused for long moments before turning to the right, and the village. Dominika would be my wife. It brought me no pleasure. I would always know how much greater my life could have been. That was the greatest curse of all.

I pulled out the trinket and tossed it in the air. Part of me still yearned to cast the bauble aside and go to the town. I wondered how I would perish if I did that. The witch's curse would be sure to make my last moments painful.

I lowered my head and stepped toward the village and the destiny that awaited me.

Strangers in the Night
Charles Williams

She captured my heart across a crowded room,
A raven-haired minx with a tall besom broom.
She returned my gaze with a come-hither look,
On the table beside her rested a large, open book.
I smiled and gave her a quick, flirting wink
And instructed the waitress to refresh her drink.
Her hennin-covered head nodded for me to join her
I took an empty seat and heard a faint, steady purr.
It was then that I noticed a black cat at her feet.
Looking deep into her eyes, my joy was complete.
She reached for my hand, and I knew it was love.
I could hear celestial choirs serenade from above.
"Let's get out here," she said. I was helpless to resist.
No greater love on this earth could ever possibly exist.
We rose as one, hand-in hand, and started to leave,
Her cat leapt from the floor and clung to her sleeve.
"I forgot my book!" she cried. I quickly rushed to retrieve.
By then my love was a raging fire and almost impossible
    to leave
I read the book's title, "Love Spells," without a trace of
    horror;
Tucking it under my arm, my love and I walked serenely
    out the door.

The Witches of Hampton Beach

Roxanne Dent

On a chilly Friday afternoon in October, I drove to Hampton Beach. I'd just inherited a two-bedroom condominium from my eccentric friend Bea. A lover of mysteries, steampunk and all things supernatural, Bea was excited about the history of the place, which she promised to share with me when I came to visit.

Busy at work, I put it off. In the interim, Bea woke up one morning, got dressed, opened the door to her deck and jumped twelve stories to the sidewalk below. She didn't leave a note. Shocked and horrified, I felt guilty for not recognizing my friend's shaky state of mind.

Neither one of us had family. I made no bones about how tired I was of renting and was saving for a down payment on a condominium. Bea knew how much I loved the ocean. It was so like her to think of me even when she must have been in pain.

In place of the modern building I envisioned, stood a garishly painted, twelve story complex. The name on the gate in front was Black Rose Court. It was old world decorated with intricate curlicues and colored verandas overlooking the sea.

Standing in front of the building were two elderly women. The taller one wore flowered, red and black, striped palazzo pants. She had short, bright red hair, beady black eyes, and a wide body. Her companion had a pointy face, a narrow neck and masses of black curls that appeared to move as if in a wind. She wore tight, black leather pants. Both had on ratty, fur coats and high heels.

As I approached the front door carrying a bag of groceries and my overnight case, leather pants stepped forward.

"Hello, dearie. My name is Myrtle. This is Babs. You must be Nadia, the new tenant in Twelve B."

"I am, but how did you—"

"Bea showed us a picture of the two of you and talked about you all the time, didn't she Babs?"

"She did."

"Your friend's death was so unexpected. Such a tragedy," Myrtle murmured.

"Every bone in her body was crushed," Babs giggled.

Myrtle stuck an elbow in her ribs

"Sad," Babs muttered.

Myrtle held out a scaly hand with long, curved, crimson nails.

I put my overnight bag down and shook hands. It was like touching dead flesh. I tried not to cringe as I withdrew my hand.

"The lawyer told us you'd be coming. We wanted to meet you in person," Myrtle said.

"But I didn't say what day I'd arrive or what time."

"We were on our way out and saw you pull up," Myrtle said.

Bab's tongue flicked out. "She's so young and delicious, isn't she, Myrtle?"

They smiled but their eyes were flat and cold.

"I own the apartment next door," Myrtle said.

"And I have the one underneath," Babs added.

"It's a quiet neighborhood. No parties, just us old fogies," Myrtle said.

"No place for a young person like you, sweetie," Babs said as she patted my shoulder.

"Babs' sister is lonely," Myrtle said. "She'd like to move in. Would you be interested in selling?"

"Daria would pay you whatever you asked," Babs assured me, as she licked her cherry, red, lips.

"I haven't even seen the place yet," I mumbled. "I'll let you know, "I added as I picked up my bag and briskly walked to the outer door, inserted the key in the lock and entered the lobby.

As I feared, the women followed me in. I stabbed the elevator button several times. Babs stood next to me.

"You won't like it here," Babs hissed.

Myrtle shoved her aside. "Babs just means it's not your kind of place. Too dull."

Relieved the old fashioned, iron cage elevator finally arrived, I practically ripped the door open and stepped inside. To my relief Myrtle and Babs remained outside. The heavy door swung shut. They glared at me in silence as the elevator slowly squeaked up.

I flipped the light switch on in the apartment and light flooded the hall and open concept living room and kitchen. I walked into the black and white kitchen, put away the groceries, removed my down jacket and made myself a cup of tea. While it heated up, I explored the apartment.

The place was spotless and smelled of lemon furniture polish and bleach. The furniture was minimal. Bea had only been here a couple of weeks and hated clutter. I was thrilled to see the two bedrooms faced the ocean and had walk-in closets. The apartment of my dreams.

The master bedroom had a stained-glass design on top of the closet door in the shape of a pentagram with a red circle in the center. It would reflect the light as it poured through the large windows in the morning.

When the tea was ready, I carried the pretty, English, flowered teacup out to the deck. A chair was already there. It was one Bea always took to the beach. I felt a stab of grief. I didn't want to cry again. I'd cried enough, and Bea would be disappointed if I didn't celebrate the generous gift she left me. I sipped the lemon ginger tea. It was one of her favorites.

The view was spectacular and the sound of the waves rising and ebbing away, along with the briny smell of the ocean was soothing. The uneasiness I felt in the women's presence dissipated. I wondered what Bea thought of her neighbors. The wind picked up. I shivered, went inside and turned up the heat.

Before I left the lawyer's office, he handed me two items, a box and Bea's diary.

"She wanted you to have these items and to tell you to double lock the front door at all times."

Surprised, I asked, *"Is it a bad neighborhood?"*

"Not that I know of, but Hampton Beach is not what it

was when I was boy. We used to leave our front doors open. Drugs are rampant and break-ins happen. You can't be too careful."

I zipped open my case, reached under all the cloths and removed the cardboard box and diary. The box was sealed with black tape.

I used a knife to open the box. Inside lay a dagger with an iron handle and a red stone in the hilt. The color matched the one above the bedroom door. On top was a paper with a title, "The Reverse Dagger," scrawled in Bea's spidery handwriting.

I chuckled. Bea loved to travel and often brought back unusual objects which she claimed were cursed or brought good luck. She didn't say where she picked up the blade. Maybe she mentioned it in her diary. It did look old. I sighed. I would miss her.

With mixed feelings, I picked up the diary. I couldn't imagine what led Bea to kill herself and wasn't sure I wanted to know, but she left her most private thoughts to me. What the hell. The least I could do was read it.

I discovered an open bottle of Bea's favorite Cabernet in the refrigerator, put on my thick, black sweater and down jacket, poured myself a glass and returned to the deck to read Bea's diary.

Bea was initially excited about purchasing the condominium for a ridiculously low price. It was a private sale from a Ukrainian gypsy who also sold her the Reverse Dagger. I smiled until I read the next line which Bea underlined. *She drowned a few days later.* Bea's excitement gradually gave way to fear and increasing paranoia.

A week after she moved in she wrote, *I can't sleep. I can't eat. I've discovered a nest of vipers and looked evil in the face. I don't know if I have the courage to do what is necessary.* On the last page, she wrote, *align the dagger with the source.*

Disturbed, I put the diary down. The sun was fading. I could no longer see the words on the page.

As I rose and turned to go inside, I glanced over the balcony. A couple of dark shadows twice the size of house cats flittered across the street. One of them stopped and looked up at me. Instinctively I leaned back out of sight.

What the hell were they? When I looked again, they were gone.

I caught sight of Myrtle in her fur coat and rubber boots as she plodded along the beach. She carried what looked like a large, white, plastic, drawstring bag and a paper bag. She reached inside the paper bag, tossed bread crumbs on the sand and was immediately surrounded by pigeons and sea gulls who fought over the crumbs. I smiled. She wasn't quite the harridan I imagined.

As one pigeon came close, she grabbed it, twisted its neck, dumped it in the plastic bag and continued on her walk as she tossed more bread crumbs.

I shuddered, went inside, shut the balcony door and locked it.Was she going to skin, grill and eat the birds? Clearly Myrtle was nuts.

I went into the master bedroom. The room was clean and neat. The cheerful, blue and white comforter was turned down and the pillows fluffed. I thought it strange if Bea planned on taking her own life, she would tidy the room and make the bed up as if she intended to return that night. After reading her diary there was no question Bea was fearful, even paranoid, but were her fears real? Was she referring to her neighbors as a nest of vipers? They were certainly bizarre but evil? When I was with her, Bea never showed any signs of paranoia. I sighed. My friend was dead, and I was no psychiatrist.

I snatched the comforter off the bed, went into the living room, wrapped myself up in it and sat in Bea's antique rocker in front of the gas fireplace. I turned the ceramic and wood lamp on and tried to erase the picture of Myrtle arriving home to chow down on sautéed pigeon as I picked up "Shroud for a Nightingale" by P.D. James.

I dozed off and awoke with a start around midnight. I had a pain in my neck and my hands were ice cold. The book was on the floor. I dragged the quilt with me, went to bed, pulled the covers up and prepared to fall back to sleep.

The sound of chanting woke me a few minutes later. I took meditation classes off and on for years, but there was something nasty about the sound of those chants that creeped me out. As I sat up, I realized they were coming from beyond the bedroom closet that connected my apartment with Myrtle's.

I started to get out of bed and stopped myself. If Myrtle and Babs decided to worship Beelzebub it was none of my business. I put my earphones in and fell into an uneasy sleep.

I awoke sometime around dawn, groggy and cranky, having vague dreams of giant monsters chasing me. I dressed in sweats and sneakers and went out for a run.

As I ran along the beach, the sun rose and warmed my back. The uneasy feelings I'd had about Bea's death, Myrtle and Babs and the house, evaporated in the light of day.

A block from my building, a fit blonde in her thirties with freckles and a ponytail jogged past me. She tripped and fell.

"Are you okay?" I asked as I reached her.

She tried to stand and winced. "Twisted my ankle."

"I'll call for a taxi," I offered as I removed my cell.

"I'll be fine," she said as she massaged her ankle. I live in that purple and pink monstrosity on the corner." She pointed to Black Rose Court.

"I was relieved to meet someone who seemed normal. "Me too. Twelve B. I just arrived yesterday. My name is Nadia."

"Julie."

"How long have you lived there?" I asked as we slowly walked back.

"A little over a year. I wanted a place by the sea and it was in my price range."

"I live next door to Myrtle. Do you know her?" I asked.

"Everyone knows Myrtle. Her friend, Babs lives across from me. I'm in 11A."

"Characters."

"Definitely, but harmless."

I thought about telling Julie about Myrtle strangling pigeons, but the incident was so bizarre I hesitated.

"You must have heard what happened to the previous owner of your place," Julie said.

"I did. It was a shock. We were friends. I inherited her condominium."

"Sorry about your friend. Are you going to stay or sell?"

"I haven't decided yet."

"It's a seller's market. You'd get a good price," she added as she limped inside and pressed for the elevator. "I know a good realter."

The elevator doors opened, and we stepped in.

"Do you like living here?" I asked.

She smiled. Her teeth were straight and so white it looked like she overdid the bleaching. "I'm a fresh air fanatic and love the sea," Julie said.

I had to ask, "Did you ever hear people chanting in the night?"

"Holly in 10C holds mediation classes every Saturday at 7:00 p.m."

"Nothing around midnight?"

"Are you kidding? Most of the tenants are retired. They're asleep by nine." Julie glanced at me. Her blue eyes lit up. "Your friend told me she collected magical objects. Did she leave you anything magical?"

The excitement and raw hunger in her blue eyes made me shake my head.

"Not unless you consider an antique rocking chair magical."

The elevator stopped.

"Nice meeting you, Julie," I said. She gave me a half smile and got off.

I watched her walk to her apartment. She was no longer limping. I'm not normally suspicious, but a part of me couldn't help thinking she deliberately tripped and fell near me in order to meet me and urge me to sell my condo. Maybe she was working with Myrtle and Babs. I chuckled at the idea of a conspiracy.

Reading Bea's diary made me paranoid. Julie was just being friendly. Like a lot of people, she was fascinated by the word magic. I stripped and stepped into a hot shower.

Relaxed after the long shower, I changed into a pair of old jeans and a comfortable, grey sweater. I opened the drawer that held the dagger and picked it up. It felt heavy. Bea wrote in her diary, *"Align the dagger with the source."*

What was the source? My eyes went to the stained-glass pentagram on top of my closet. The sun streamed through the wall of windows and the red stone glowed.

Instinct made me point the dagger at the red stone in the pentagram. Writing appeared on the dark oak wood floor:

From Dust to Dawn
Lords of Darkness
Beasts from Ancient Times
Return to the pits
Of Mud and Slime

The bell rang and startled me. I put the dagger away and locked the drawer. The writing faded away. I went to the front door and opened it. On the floor in front of my door was a dead pigeon, its head sliced off.

I stormed over and banged on Myrtle's door. I was met with silence. "Bitches," I shouted.

How dare Myrtle try to scare me into selling. I dumped the carcass in the garbage and tossed it down the chute. Myrtle was unhinged and possibly dangerous, but if I reported the incident to the police, and she denied the whole thing, I had no proof. It was only my word she strangled those pigeons on the beach. It might not even be illegal.

I went inside and slammed the door. I paced around the apartment for ten minutes inundated with questions. Why would Myrtle go to such lengths? Just so Babs' sister could move in? There was something else going on.

I'm not a student of magic but I'd say The Reverse Dagger qualified as a magical item. Was that why Julie wanted to know if I had it? Did the tenants of Black Rose Court belong to an evil witches' cult? Bea mentioned a nest of vipers.

I removed a deck of playing cards I'd brought and began to shuffle. It calmed me and let me focus. Did the Ukrainian woman drown on her own or was she punished for breaking some rule by selling the apartment out from under them and giving Bea the Reverse Dagger? And was Bea's death a suicide or was she pushed off the deck? The whole idea of a house full of devil cult murderers was crazy. I made sure the front door was double-locked.

I wasn't hungry. I scrambled a couple of eggs and

nibbled a piece of burnt toast. When I finished eating, I tried reading but every little sound, ice dropping in the refrigerator, or a car backfiring outside unnerved me. I turned the television on and watched a nature show about the snub-nosed monkeys of Shangri-La. By the time it was done it was dark out and I called it a night.

Awakened at midnight by deep throated chants coming from the closet that made me want to scream, I jumped out of bed, ran into the living room, unlocked the drawer and removed the Reverse Dagger. If a bunch of loonies were practicing black magic, and murdered Bea, I felt safer with a blade in my hand. I padded over to the closet in bare feet and pjs and entered.

The chants were stronger inside the closet. A powerful red beam began to pulse above me.I glanced up and ducked as the red stone in the center of the pentagram above my door burst into a whirling vortex.

Something huge, dark and scaly howled as it flashed by me. The chants in Myrtle's apartment abruptly stopped as whatever the dark form was spun through the pentagram on my side and crashed into Myrtle's. The vortex closed, leaving only the pentagram.

I told myself to mind my own business, but the time for that was when I first woke up and heard the chants. Curiosity was always my downfall. I couldn't go back without knowing what the hell was going on.

I moved closer to the connecting wall.

The thing that tore its way into Myrtle's apartment broke the door on my side. Myrtle's closet was crammed with clothes, boxes and junk. I stepped over her jumbled dresses and furs. The stench was foul. I tried not to sneeze as the dust settled over me, although I doubted anyone would hear me in the racket Myrtle and the others were making in her bedroom. I moved closer to the door that led to her bedroom and peered through the opening made by whatever crashed through.

The room was crowded, but not by humans. I clamped a hand over my mouth to keep from screaming.

"Another dark lord joins us. Give him air," Myrtle's voice rang out. Her true form was that of a behemoth toad with giant, black wings that puffed out with excitement. Her long tongue was covered with lumps and sores and her bulbous, black eyes bulged out of a hideous mingling of toad and human features. In her excitement, her tongue flew out and she swallowed one of the dead pigeons lying on a silver platter.

The slithering, black cats I'd seen on the street hissed and screeched as they squirmed on the floor. Other loathsome creatures, only seen in horror flicks or medieval books on Hell crowded round, paying homage to the new beast. In the middle stood, Myrtle and Babs.

"Welcome, Lord Angra Mainyu," Babs shouted. Her hair was alive with hissing rattlesnakes. Her red lips dripped with blood. I realized with horror, the creature that loomed next to her was Julie, no longer the perky, freckle faced blonde, but a large, black spider whose face retained few human features of the runner on the beach.

I dragged my eyes away as my attention was drawn to the abomination that suddenly rose up from the floor. Its enormous, scaly head brushed the eight-foot ceiling. I could smell its feted breath from my hiding place.

The head sported long, green horns and its red eyes glowed with evil as it scanned the room. It had a long tail and a scaly, dark body the color of dried blood. Each step it took caused the room to shake and its long, sharp claws left deep incisions on the wood floor. One of the wriggling, cat-like creatures squealed as it failed to move quick enough and was crushed under the beast's feet.

I stumbled over the clothes and fell. Every nerve in me wanted to run out of the building and keep on running. Sheer terror froze me to the spot. If I broke the pentagram in both Myrtle's closet and mine it would stop any more beasts from coming through, but the ones here would remain in our world. I realized with horror I needed to destroy them all.

My hand that held the dagger was sweaty and hot. The words, "Align the dagger with the source," was obvious now. The pentagram was the source. I had the dagger. But would the words work to send the demons back where they came from? I heard movement and scrambled to the back just as the closet door swung open.

Myrtle reached in with arms that were covered in bumpy flesh. I held my breath, but she didn't notice me behind all the hanging and discarded clothes. She began to sing to herself as she knocked over boxes and hopped about.

"Greasy grime and gopher guts—"

She stopped singing and sniffed the air. I prayed I wouldn't sneeze. She returned to her singing. "Mutilated monkey meat—

Yanking a box from above, she grunted, kicked the door shut with a spade-like back foot

and left me in darkness.

What if I couldn't remember the exact words of the spell? Or I was missing some important detail? I shoved clothes which smelled strongly of sulphur and mildew off me. I couldn't stay here forever. The ruckus in the bedroom was quieter now. I cracked the closet door open a fraction of an inch and peered out. The creatures had moved from the bedroom into the hall. I could hear Myrtle's voice and see her hideous form reflected in the mirror on the wall.

"We agreed not to expose ourselves to humans until midnight on Halloween when the vortex will open permanently, and all our brothers and sisters will come through. Those who disobey must be punished. You were seen on the beach, Moog."

The remaining cat-like creature tried to slither away.

"Get him," Myrtle shouted. Her tongue rolled out of her mouth and her bat wings puffed up in a frenzy of excitement as she jumped up and down on a hall table as the cat screeched. The dragon descended on the creature and ripped him apart with claws and teeth, tossing body parts to the crowd. I could hear bones crack and break.

This was the perfect moment when they were all together and focused on their gory feast. I slipped out of the closet. My knees felt rubbery and I couldn't control the shakes. On the positive side, no one had seen me yet.

I held the Reverse Dagger up and pointed the tip to line up with the pentagrams. I softly chanted the words to the spell, fearful of attracting the attention of the demons. I needn't have worried. The noise level in the hall was raucous.

I raised my voice, "From Dust to Dawn, Lords of Darkness, Beasts from Ancient Times," I began and felt a surge of power pulse through my arm. The red stone in the center of the pentagram began to glow and spin. The vortex opened and bathed the bedroom and hall with a blood-red glow.

Myrtle spotted me and screeched, "The bitch has the Reverse Dagger. Kill her."

I shut my eyes and raised my voice as I finished the spell, "Return to the Pits of Mud and
Slime."

I felt the floor shake and knew the dragon lord led the pack of shrieking fiends to me. Sharp talons dug into my flesh. I screamed but didn't let go.

The power of the spell worked its magic. The ancient beasts were sucked into the vortex, their unholy screams echoing in the room long after they'd vanished.

I collapsed weak with relief and loss of blood. I wasn't done yet. I entered the kitchen and rummaged through drawers until I found a steel mallet. I dragged a chair into the bedroom and placed it in front of the closet, climbed up and smashed the glass pentagram on Myrtle's side. When I was done, I returned to my apartment and did the same with the one on my side.

After washing and bandaging my arm, I swept up all the glass and dumped it down the chute.

The sun rose and filled my living room with light. I opened the sliding doors to the balcony and stepped outside. The sky was blue. It was Sunday. Church bells began to ring all over town. The sound reverberated through the streets as if declaring, "Ding dong, the witch is dead."

Recipes from Granny's Kitchen

If you are looking for delicious, low fat recipes—this ain't it.

While only one or two of the recipes listed below are mentioned in my short story, The Whisperer, I wanted to throw in some others. What you will see below is a bunch of good old Southern recipes and they are rich and hearty. These are the kinds of things that would have been found on my own grandmother's table. She always cooked enough for an army because the Story family is large and prone to drop in for a meal at any given time. Kids, grandkids, cousins, neighbors—it didn't matter. Everyone was welcome at Granny's table.

I like to think she used a little magick in everything she cooked on that old wood-burning stove.

Now, I'm sharing a few of those with you in what I think would be a typical meal for my granny.

Enjoy.

5-Hour Beef Stew
Ingredients
4 lbs round steak or brisket (Sprinkle liberally with meat tenderizer and allow to sit for about an hour before cooking; then cut into chunks.)
6 beef bouillon cubes
2 small onions, diced
5 stalks celery, chopped
2 lbs carrots, chopped
1 cup tapioca pearls (Granulated tapioca actually works better these days. This works to thicken the stew.)
1 ½ quarts tomato juice
10 to 12 medium potatoes cut into chunks
Salt and pepper to taste

Directions
Put all ingredients into a large roaster pan. Cover and bake up to (You guessed it!) five hours at 250 degrees. This makes a lot. Invite some people over.

Cauliflower Salad
Ingredients
1 head of lettuce (chopped)
1 head of cauliflower (chopped)
1 lb. of bacon (fried until crisp, then crumbled when cooled)
1 onion (chopped)

Dressing for salad
2 cups mayonnaise
½ cup grated parmesan cheese
½ cup sugar
(If this is too sweet—¼ cup grated parmesan cheese and 1/3 cup sugar)

Directions
Layer salad ingredients in a bowl and then spread prepared dressing on top. DO NOT toss ingredients together until ready to serve or the lettuce will begin to go limp. It can be made the day before it's needed and refrigerated overnight. When ready to serve, toss ingredients until well mixed.

Sour Cream Corn Bread

Ingredients
1 ½ cups self-rising corn meal
1 cup vegetable oil
2 Tbsp. sugar
2 eggs
1 small can cream style corn
1 small (8 oz.) carton sour cream

Directions
Mix all ingredients together and pour into greased muffin pans. Cook 40 minutes at 400 degrees

Chess Pie
(Buttery and rich, this simple pie is a Southern classic.)

Ingredients
3 eggs (beaten)
1 ½ cups sugar
½ cup melted butter
2 Tbsp. buttermilk
2 Tsp. vanilla
1 pie crust

Directions
Preheat oven to 350 degrees. Combine all ingredients (except the pie crust) in a large mixing bowl and beat until well mixed. Pour into the pie crust and bake at 350 degrees for 45 to 60 minutes. Start checking on the pie at 45 minutes—inserting a knife or toothpick in the center -- You will know the pie is done when the knife or toothpick comes out clean.
*** Note: I put the pie on a cookie sheet before placing it in the oven, in case of overspill while baking.*

Who?

Anatoly Belilovsky was born in a city that went through six or seven owners in the last century, all of whom used it to do a lot more than drive to church on Sundays; he is old enough to remember tanks rolling through it on their way to Czechoslovakia in 1968. After being traded to the US for a shipload of grain and a defector to be named later, he learned English from Star Trek reruns and went on to become a pediatrician in an area of New York where English is only the fourth most commonly used language. He has neither cats nor dogs, but was admitted into SFWA in spite of this deficiency, having published original and translated stories in NATURE, F&SF, Daily SF, Kasma, UFO, Stupefying Stories, Cast of Wonders, and other markets. He blogs about writing at loldoc.net.

Tyree Campbell has long established himself as a well-respected and award-winning writer, editor, talented linguist, limerick aficionado, coffee snob, and seeker of budding talent. If you haven't read one of his vast number of novels or stories—then why haven't you? No, seriously. Why haven't you? Go do it now. You will find him lurking about Facebook's Alban Lake Publishing page.

Sarah Cannavo's poems and short stories have appeared

in venues like *Carrying On, Untimely Frost, Parody, Poetry Quarterly, Postcards From the Void, Schlock! Horror!, Darkling's Beasts and Brews, The Devil's Hour, It Came From the Garage!, The Literary Hatchet*, and *Liminality*, and her poem "The 5 Stages of Being on Hold" won third place in the 2018 Wergle Flomp Humor Poetry Contest. Upcoming stories will appear in *Deranged* and *Rope Burns*. Recent projects include finishing a novel for the first time in for-ever and putting together her first collection of poetry. She sometimes manages to write about these and other projects on her site, The Moody Muse (www.moodilymusing.blogspot.com) or rant about them on Twitter @moodilymusing.

Nicola Currie's work will be recognized with the poem, Tickle, Tickle, Burn, Burn. This UK writer's poem fit the theme perfectly for this anthology, as well as being just plain fun to read.

Claire Davon has written on and off for most of her life, starting with fan fiction when she was very young. She writes across a wide range of genres, and does not consider any of it off limits. Her novels can be found in the paranormal romance and contemporary romance sections, while her short stories run the gamut. If a story calls to her, she will write it. She currently lives in Los Angeles and spends her free time writing novels and short stories, as well as doing animal rescue and enjoying the sunshine.

Roxanne Dent lives in Massachusetts and has sold nine novels and dozens of short stories in a variety of genres, including Paranormal Fantasy, Regency, Mystery, Horror, Steampunk, Drabbles, Middle Grade and YA. She has also co-authored short stories and plays with her sister, Karen Dent, written screenplays and wrote and directed her own three-minute thriller which won the "Audience Choice Awards in the Bare Bones International Film Festival. Member of New England Horror Writers, Essex Writers and Artists Guild, Fiction Writers Guild and The Berlin Writers Group.

E.M. Eastick is a writer from Australia. Eastick's poem, The Flying Spell, is clever, fun, and absolutely delightful to read.

C. I. I. Jones is a Virginia writer whose story, Both Sides Now, will leave you with goosebumps.

Ngo Binh Anh Khoa is a teacher of English in Ho Chi Minh city, Vietnam who is also addicted to perusing fictions and poetry in his free time. His poems have previously been featured in Eternal Haunted Summer, Star*Line, NewMyths, Heroic Fantasy Quarterly, The Audient Void and other venues.

Gregory Norris grew up on a healthy diet of creature double features and classic SF TV. Among the witchiest of his favorites was Burn, Witch, Burn, Dark Shadows, and the "The Trevi Collection" episode of The Night Stalker. He penned the first draft of "The Salted Circle" at a retreat center for writers in the remote Vermont countryside, a place that doubles for the setting of his story. Follow his literary adventures at www.gregorylnorris.blogspot.com.

James Pate has been published at Black Warrior Review, New Delta Review, Occulum, Superstition Review and Berkeley Fiction Review, among other places. His collection of essays on contemporary Gothic poetry, entitled Flowers Among the Carrion, was published by Actions Books in 2016. His occult noir novel Speed of Life was published by Fahrenheit Press in 2017. He is currently working on a novel about a cult in New Orleans.

Terrie Leigh Relf, AKA The Boortean Ambassador to Haura, is currently in orbit over Ocean Beach, an intriguing community located in San Diego, California. She enjoys walking along the shore, as well as the Ocean Beach Pier, where some Haurans often see UFOs and other "supposedly" unexplained phenomena. When she's not seeking inspiration (or contact with other visitors) along Haura's coastal regions, Relf serves as the contest judge and editor for the somewhat quarterly Alban Lake

Publishing drabble contests. Relf also serves on a variety of Alban Lake Publishing's special projects committees, and is the poetry editor for Tales from the Moonlit Path. You can learn more about her at https://tlrelf.wordpress.com/, http://terrieleighrelf.com/ and https://tlrelfreikipractitioner.wordpress.com/.

L.A. Story -- A resident of Northeast Mississippi, L.A. (Lee Ann) Story is a professional, independent author with the Mid-South Authors' Co-op, having published five novels, two short stories, and a novella under their imprint - River Oaks Press. Her short stories and poetry have been widely published by many magazines and anthologies. She is also a frequent guest editor for various projects for Alban Lake Publishing. Among her most recent honors, she is a 2019 Darrell Award Finalist. She is also freelance writer and columnist for the Daily Corinthian. Although born in Tennessee, she is a naturalized Mississippian who lives in an enchanted wood. For more information about L.A. Story and her work, visit her website at: www.lastorywriter.com.

Charlie Williams is a retired teacher living in Oakdale, California, with his wife and their two canine children. Two of his short stories have been accepted by "Stupefying Stories" and "The NoSleep Podcast". In addition to his writing projects, he is currently assisting a former student with his horror-themed podcasts and film productions.